Dear America

The Diary of
Margaret Ann Brady

Voyage on
the Great Titanic

ELLEN EMERSON WHITE

SCHOLASTIC INC. • NEW YORK

For Holly

The Library of Congress has catalogued the earlier hardcover edition as follows:
White, Ellen Emerson.
Voyage on the great Titanic : the diary of Margaret Ann Brady, R.M.S. Titanic,
1912 / Ellen Emerson White.   p . cm.   — (Dear America)
Summary: In her diary in 1912, thirteen-year-old Margaret Ann describes how
she leaves her lonely life in a London orphanage to become a companion to a
wealthy American woman, sails on the Titanic, and experiences its sinking.
ISBN 0-590-96273-6
1. Titanic (Steamship)—Juvenile fiction. [1. Titanic (Steamship)—Fiction.
2. Shipwrecks—Fiction. 3. Ocean liners—Fiction. 4. Orphans—Fiction. 5. London
(England)—Fiction. 6. Diaries—Fiction.] I. Title. II. Series.
PZ7.W58274Vo 1998
[Fic]—dc21   98-27501   CIP   AC

Trade Paper-Over-Board edition ISBN 978-0-545-23834-2
Reinforced Library edition ISBN 978-0-545-26235-4

10 9 8 7 6 5 4 3 2 1   10 11 12 13 14

The text type was set in ITC Legacy Serif.
The display type was set in Amazone.
Book design by Kevin Callahan

Printed in the U.S.A.   23
This edition first printing, November 2010

London,
England

1912

Thursday, 28 March 1912

St. Abernathy's Orphanage for Girls
Whitechapel, London, England

I feel rather a fool writing down my thoughts, but this evening, Sister Catherine made the very firm suggestion that I start keeping a diary—and handed me a brand-new tablet from the supply closet for that very purpose. She says that everything has changed for me now, and I will be disappointed later if I do not keep a written record. Failing that, she assured me that *she* would be disappointed. In all honesty, I so prefer to guard my privacy that I do not think I would accept such a directive from anyone else, but my fondness for her is such that it seems only proper to follow her advice. In any case, there is no question but that today was nothing if not eventful. One moment, my life was mundane; mere hours later, the whole world seemed new and different.

It was midmorning, and I was in the midst of a clumsy declamation—"'Tyger! Tyger! burning bright/In the forests of the night,'"—when I was summoned to Sister Mary Gregoria's office.

I went with great uneasiness, as I had been some-what unruly at breakfast, and would now almost certainly have to serve my penance in the form of . . . chores.

"Margaret Ann!" Sister Mary Gregoria said, her voice surely as loud as Bow bells. She waved a piece of paper at me, and then pointed at the chair where she wanted me to sit.

I have been known to post a solemn note here and there in the common rooms, proposing pecu-liar new policies, and scrawling a facsimile of Sister Mary Gregoria's signature below, but this sheet did not look familiar. It would be a shame to be pun-ished for the offense of another — and yet, truth be told, probably not altogether undeserved.

Then Sister Catherine bustled in, murmuring an apology for her tardiness. Obviously, she and I are close, so I sensed that whatever punishment I was getting this time would not be too severe.

When I first came here, some five years ago, I do not think I spoke at all for several months. It was a dark and unhappy time, and I rarely ate, or slept through the night. I was assigned, as my regular task, to assist a Sister Catherine in the library. During those early days, I felt shy around the jolly, stout woman in the sweeping black habit, but soon I grew to depend on her kindnesses. When I felt most alone, she would always be there with a smile, a book she thought I might enjoy, and a hot cup of sweet, milky tea. Now, that small, book-cluttered room is the one place in the world that feels like home to me. Sister Catherine is very wise, and has guided my studies far beyond my basic classwork, with the hope that I might even attend university one day. Other than my brother, William, I believe she is my favorite person.

"Margaret Ann," Sister Mary Gregoria said again, once Sister Catherine had settled herself upon a flimsy wooden chair. "I am told that it is your wish to go into service."

I *want* to do no such thing, but neither do I fancy ending up back in the back alleys of Whitechapel, or even worse, in a workhouse. So I nodded in a grave manner. William has been trying to save enough money to secure my passage to America for nigh on two years now. If I were also able to work,

I could help with my fair share. William is the only family I have in the world, and I am eager to join him over there.

"Should you like to be a companion, Margaret Ann?" Sister Mary Gregoria asked.

Since I was not sure what that meant, I did not know how to respond.

"This will give you so many more opportunities," Sister Catherine said, her face bright with happiness. "It is exactly what I would have wished for you, Margaret."

I knew that she would only tell me the truth, so I nodded. Then I turned to look at Sister Mary Gregoria and presented her with a very large smile. "I should *love* to be a companion," I said.

And so it was that I set forth to the City that afternoon, with Sister Catherine as my chaperon.

The hour grows late, and I am tired, so I think I will tell of our City adventure in the morning.

St. Abernathy's Orphanage for Girls
Whitechapel

None of the Sisters felt I ought to be wandering about the streets by myself, which was why Sister Catherine was to accompany me. There was great concern about what I should wear on our jaunt to the City, since they wanted very much for me to make a good impression. As a rule, the Sisters' only concern is that our clothing is *clean*. We wear very plain, simple dresses, and do our best to keep them in good condition. Some of the merchants in Petticoat Lane donate their castoffs to the orphanage, but they are, of course, not top-quality garments. In the end, it was decided that I would wear a dark blue frock, which once belonged to one of the older girls. Sister Celeste arranged my hair neatly, and I used a soft cloth to rub a bit of shine into my button-boots.

Perhaps it goes without saying that Sister Catherine wore her habit.

I was eager to take the Underground, since I

have scarcely ever traveled that way, but instead, we rode on a motor bus to Piccadilly Circus. Sister Catherine was strangely nervous and silent, so I spent my time staring out the window. When I was very small, Mummy and Father would take us to the City once in a great while. I remember a picnic in Regent's Park, and another day, when we stood and stared at Buckingham Palace with great admiration.

Piccadilly was crowded with enticing food stalls, street performers, and other lovely sights. I was very hungry, and the vendors' cries of "'ot meat pies!" and "Taters! All 'ot!" made my stomach rumble. Many a man passing by raised his hat to Sister Catherine and murmured, "Afternoon, Sister," before continuing on his way.

Sister Catherine was very concerned that we would lose our way, and she stopped to ask a bobby for directions. I knew only that we were going to a fine hotel in Mayfair to meet a rich American lady for tea.

We walked for several blocks, turning right and left and right again. I wanted to tarry on Savile Row, to scrutinize the windows of its exclusive clothing stores, but Sister Catherine felt that we had no time to linger. As we walked vigorously, I enjoyed watching the fine ladies and gentlemen strolling about, with pretty parasols and mahogany walking sticks. The ladies wore the most astonishing hats! Perhaps my frock *was* too humble for the likes of Mayfair.

The name of the hotel was Claridge's, and it looked so fancy that I was shy about going inside. Sister Catherine had stopped, so perhaps she felt timid, too.

"Margaret Ann," she said, sounding terribly serious. "I must remind you that there are times when it is best to sit quietly, and merely listen."

I am afraid I am often so eager to be clever, that I speak without thinking. When Sister Catherine is cross, she calls me "Saucy Girl." This always makes me laugh, and then she is even more cross.

"Nary a word," I promised.

"Remember, she is American," Sister Catherine said. "Be kind."

I nodded. I have heard that Americans have simply dreadful accents, and tend to be lacking in characteristics like reserve and dignity. I decided, for the time being, to suspend my judgment.

Two young men in elegant uniforms stood at either side of the entrance to the hotel. When they saw us, they promptly swung the great doors open and ushered us inside. I must admit, I felt like a princess.

Never had I been in such luxurious surroundings! The floors were of marble so shiny, I do believe I could see my own reflection in them. A beautiful staircase loomed ahead of us, and the ceiling sparkled with chandeliers.

Sister Catherine asked another uniformed man to direct us to the Foyer, where we were to meet Mrs. Frederick Carstairs for tea. The man bowed and motioned for us to come along.

We were taken into a lovely room where a quartet was playing *live* music! Everywhere, ladies sat at small, exquisite tables, while graceful footmen served them tea. The air was filled with the sounds of chamber music, delicate china clinking, and soft conversations.

We were led to a table, where a plump, middle-aged woman sat. She was wearing an ornate flowery hat, a boxy dress, and long gloves, all in various shades of minty green. Something about her posture put me in mind of a spring pigeon. Seeing us, she lowered her glasses and looked me over with a critical eye.

"Mrs. Carstairs, I am Sister Catherine from St. Abernathy's," Sister Catherine said, "and may I present Miss Margaret Ann Brady."

Mrs. Carstairs studied me, and then extended her hand. I was startled by her forwardness, but then reminded myself that she was, after all, American, and forced myself to return the gesture. She gave my hand an abrupt shake, then dropped it.

"I am very pleased to meet you, Mrs. Carstairs," I said, as polite as can be. I noticed, then, that she was holding a small, and rather smug, brown terrier. Although I prefer cats, I am terribly fond of all animals. "What a delightful pet," I said, and reached out to stroke her.

"Don't!" Mrs. Carstairs said sharply, her voice loud enough to make me wince. "She doesn't take to strangers!"

By then, the dog was already licking my hand. Mrs. Carstairs seemed surprised, but not displeased; Sister Catherine had the exact opposite reaction. Once we were seated, and Mrs. Carstairs had told me that the dog's name was Florence, one of the uniformed footmen appeared with a steaming teapot to fill our cups.

I had never seen such a glorious tea! Plate upon plate of small sandwiches, crumpets, scones, cakes, and petits fours. I am always hungry — Sister Catherine says I grow an inch every fortnight — and I wanted to eat my fill, then gather up the rest to bring back to Nora, who is the youngest child at St. Abernathy's, and to whom I am quite partial.

Mrs. Carstairs nibbled a bite of sandwich here, a taste of shortbread there. I tried to make each half sandwich last for three full bites, though I could easily have popped them into my mouth whole. But I knew my manners would reflect upon Sister Catherine, and so I endeavored to be discreet.

Cucumber, salmon, roast beef, watercress, a soft white cheese, thinly sliced ham — the sandwich varieties seemed endless. If you began to empty your plate, the cheerful footman appeared at once to replace it. Because of this, I liked him very much, and smiled broadly at him each time.

"How ever do you stay so slim?" Mrs. Carstairs asked, by and by, her voice a bit stiff.

I took this as a hint to restrain myself, although Sister Catherine sprang to my defense with her "inch a fortnight" explanation. This was followed by a brief discussion of how tall I am for my age, and Mrs. Carstairs seemed somewhat dismayed to discover that I am only thirteen. Sister Catherine instantly assured her that I have always been mature beyond my years, although I will concede that there are times when that is probably debatable.

"I am surprised to find your accent so refined," Mrs. Carstairs said, seeming now to remember that I was at the table. "You sound very learned."

Although I had been silent for quite some time, I, naturally, assumed that meant she wanted to hear a somewhat learned remark. "'Oh, to be in England/ Now that April's there,'" I responded.

"Ah," Mrs. Carstairs said, although she looked uncomfortable.

It was quiet for a moment, and then she asked if that was Keats. I thought surely she was having a bit of fun with me, until Sister Catherine said softly, "Robert Browning." Mrs. Carstairs gave that some consideration, then remarked upon the fine job the Sisters had done of educating me.

In truth, I can rip out a right impressive string of Cockney — as only befits one born in Wapping — that would singe the ears of a sailor, but I have also never found it difficult to mimic the accents of others. Mummy always said I had a fine ear, and might well be musical, were I ever to get the opportunity to learn an instrument. The pianoforte, she hoped. I enjoy music, and would have been happy with a mouth organ. Once, Father found me a penny-whistle, upon which I blew nonstop until Mummy decided to "put it away" for a time.

Father had a beautiful light brogue, and often when we spoke, I would lapse into my own. This gave him no end of amusement, and, I hope, pleasure. He was very proud of his roots — County Cork, in Ireland, to be sure — and told me many wonderful stories about the old country, and the wondrous sights to be found there.

Sister Eulalia, who grew up a very proper

young lady in Kensington, has always been very strict about our pronunciation. "H's!" she says in snappish tones. "I want to hear your H's!" Then one of my classmates will promptly say, "Sure, and h'it's an 'eavenly diy h'out, h'it 'tis." Whereupon, Sister Eulalia puts her head upon her desk. Often, I cannot resist speaking to her in the broadest, most mangled Cockney imaginable. She tells me that I am very, very wicked, and then slaps a ruler across my knuckles to punctuate the scolding.

This may not bode well for my future as a pianoforte virtuoso.

"You have a pleasant demeanor," Mrs. Carstairs said then, "but I sense some mischief about you."

I wanted to laugh, but knew that would only confirm her suspicions. So I lowered my head in a shy manner, and quietly sipped some tea. I was still very hungry, but confined myself to a small piece of sponge cake.

After a time, it was decided that I should take Florence for a short walk, while Sister Catherine and Mrs. Carstairs spoke privately. The dog, I saw now, wore a jeweled collar, and a light pink silken lead. I took her out through the opulent lobby, and we wandered up to Bond Street before returning. Florence had a sprightly gait, and seemed to enjoy barking at everyone — and every*thing* — we passed. I cannot imagine why she, for example, found the gas lamps objectionable. But, to her credit, she was a spirited animal, if foolishly small.

When we returned to the Foyer, Sister Catherine and Mrs. Carstairs were still speaking in low, serious voices.

". . . remarkably bright child," Sister Catherine was saying, "and very congenial."

Given the charming tenor of the conversation, I was loathe to interrupt. However, they stopped at once when they saw me. Upon entering the hotel, Florence had jumped up into my arms, where she was now lounging happily. Mrs. Carstairs looked at us, and seemed to make up her mind.

"Margaret Ann, would you like to go to America?" she asked.

I wanted nothing more! "I should be delighted," I said.

Saturday, 30 March 1912

St. Abernathy's Orphanage for Girls
Whitechapel

I simply cannot sleep tonight. Earlier, I wrote to William to tell him the wonderful news, and Sister Mary Gregoria is to post the letter in the morning. I feel very lucky, and yet also frightened. I have grown used to my life here, and am not sure I am ready for so many changes all at once.

Mrs. Carstairs and I are to sail for America, ten days hence, on a ship called the RMS *Titanic*. RMS means Royal Mail Steamer, Sister Catherine told me later. Before we left the hotel, Mrs. Carstairs gave me all the details of our upcoming journey, and what she will expect of me. Mainly, I gather, I am to be polite and agreeable — and to fetch and carry and otherwise help out with whatever she needs at any given point in time. I assured her that I would have no problem complying with these rules, although I am afraid her loud tones will grate on me. Naturally, I did not share this concern.

Mrs. Carstairs is terribly excited about being

aboard this particular ship, as it is the *Titanic*'s maiden voyage, and she is supposed to be the finest ocean liner in the world, as well as the largest ever built. I know nothing of ships, and see no reason to doubt her. I gather Mr. and Mrs. Carstairs have been sailing the Atlantic for many years, and have been on all of the great liners, including the *Titanic*'s sister ship, the *Olympic*.

Originally, they were to make this trip together, along with Mr. Carstairs's — one assumes, faithful — manservant. Hence, they had reserved two cabins on the ship. But now, Mr. Carstairs has been detained here in the City on business, and so will rejoin his wife in a month or two. Their daughter, it turns out, has only just given birth to their first grandchild, a boy named Theodore, and Mrs. Carstairs wants to see him as soon as possible. Mr. Carstairs did not want her to travel by herself, which is why they decided to seek out a companion.

I am still not quite sure how this fortunate assignment came my way. I believe there may have been an advertisement, but an "East End-ing" acquaintance of the Carstairs' may have brought St. Abernathy's to their attention. Now and again, with a desire to do good works, fancy London ladies come to this neighborhood to tutor poor urchins, and otherwise provide enrichment and counsel to the destitute. The ladies call this "East End-ing," and sometimes, less politely, "slumming." Most of their charitable time is given to the better-known missions and settlement houses, like Toynbee Hall. But every so often, they come across our small orphanage, too. I suppose there are some who are awed by, and overcome with gratitude for, these earnest, well-to-do ladies, but I tend not to be among them. Somehow, I have never fancied being the object of pity.

And yet, in many ways, I suppose our situation here *is* rather pitiful. The nuns have limited funds, and we are always overcrowded. Right now, there are at least twenty other girls sleeping here in the tiny dormitory — one of three in the orphanage — and it can be very loud. The room can barely hold ten beds, so we have makeshift double bunks. Nora, who is only five, sleeps below me. I know she would rather have the upper bunk, but she is so often troubled by nightmares that I fear she would fall out and hurt herself.

There is a window just above my bunk, and when sleep will not come, I like to look out at the lively streets below. Whitechapel is never still, and there are always people to see. There is a public house 'round the corner, and I am particularly fond of listening to the sounds of music and laughter.

I was not quite eight years old when I came here. No, the true story is that William *left* me here, one cold and desperate night some five years ago.

When my family lived in Wapping, near the river, we were happy. We rented the bottom half of a cottage, which had two small rooms separated by a muslin curtain. Father worked very hard as a labourer on the London Docks. When times were good, he helped load cargo; when work was scarce, he would toil as a coal-whipper, and come home black with soot. Mummy was always frail, but she took in sewing when she was able. She was consumptive, and I would often wake in the night to her muffled coughing. We worried about her greatly, but in the daylight hours, she always had a smile for us.

I suppose we were poor, but we never went without food. There was little money to spare, but Father always made sure that Mummy had her tea with sugar, and that William and I had a glass of milk to drink. Once in a very great while, we would get to feast on fish and chips, all bundled up in newspaper. I don't know that there is any food I love more than fresh, "'ot" chips. After supper, Mummy would smooth out the newspapers and blot away the worst of the oil so she could read whatever was beneath. I remember her helping me with my letters and numbers, and later, we would read together for hours.

One icy February afternoon, three burly men came to the door, twisting their wool hats in their hands, and avoiding Mummy's eyes. A great load of crates had come crashing down at the Docks, and although Father was able to push another worker out of the way, he could not save himself. They were sore sorry, the men said, shuffling their boots.

Mummy did her best to keep the family together. She began working in the rag trade, and was gone from sunrise to sunset, sewing buttons in a hot, airless factory. She grew very thin, and we rarely saw more than a shadow of her old smile. Then, early the next spring, she took ill. Her fever raged, and William and I did not know what to do, other than make tea and try to feed her digestives. By the time Mr. Harris, who lived down the way, brought a doctor — a grey-faced little man dressed in a black suit — it was too late.

These are hard memories, and I will save the rest of the story for another time.

Sunday, 31 March 1912
St. Abernathy's Orphanage for Girls
Whitechapel

Today was a quiet day, as Sundays generally are. We go to a very long mass in the morning, eat a substantial midday meal, and then have free time until our early evening tea. I spent most of the afternoon glancing through *A Midsummer Night's Dream*, and trying not to think too much. I am to return to Claridge's later this week, as Mrs. Carstairs has concerns about my wardrobe, and wishes to have me fitted for "appropriate" clothing. That seems like a frightful waste of money to me, but I have been told not to concern myself with such matters. I gather that neither money, nor the lack thereof, are problems for the Carstairs. I would far prefer to wear the clothes I have, but when I broached this to Sister Catherine, she just sighed, and said, "Be agreeable."

As I sit here in the library, thinking about the future, I cannot help also remembering the past. In his letters, William speaks about the Colonies in glowing descriptions, but I am still feeling a trifle hesitant. I scarcely know Mrs. Carstairs, and if we don't get on, the voyage could be difficult. For *both* of us. I suppose, though, I can occupy myself with Florence.

But this journey can only be easy, compared to the horrible days after Mummy's death, when William and I were on our own. For a time, we were able to stay with the McDougals, who lived three streets down. I knew two of their daughters from the ragged school. The McDougals' small rooms were crowded, so William and I each slept in a burlap sack, on the floor near the woodstove. Food was scarce, and William did what he could to provide for us, so that we would not be a burden. I know he resorted to stealing more often than not, but if

I asked him, he would get very angry, and I learned to avoid the subject.

Mr. McDougal and his brother Kieran spent many an hour at the public houses, and would come home much the worse for drink. They would be spoiling for a fight, and Mr. McDougal would swing out a big hand at anyone who looked at him cross-eyed. After I got knocked down a time or two, William grew to fear for my safety, and packed up our few possessions one morning and took us away.

But, of course, we had no place to go. We lived on the streets, sleeping in alcoves and doorways, or anyplace we could find shelter. Sometimes, we were able to earn a few shillings by mud-larking — exploring the riverbanks and wading into the filthy water, trying to find objects we could sell. Lumps of coal, lengths of rope, broken crates — *anything* that someone else might want. While William tried to interest passersby in our gatherings, I would crawl under the stalls in the market, looking for discarded food. Sometimes I might be lucky and find a squashed orange, or heel of bread, but other days, we lived on rather foul scraps or — far too often — went hungry.

I think it was December — we had long since lost track of the days — when hard sleet fell all one day and night. Though I was terribly ill with a fever and hacking cough, I was afraid to go to hospital. William wanted to take me to a charity orphanage for girls some mate had told him about, but I refused. We had had this argument before, and I had no intention of being separated from him — he was all I had left. He threatened to *make* me go, and I said he would have to round up every bobby in London to do the job — and even then I did not like his chances. In the meantime, the sleet faded into damp fog, and then back to bone-chilling sleet. We huddled in an alley, with me trying not to weep between bouts of shivering and coughing.

"That's it," he said suddenly. He stuffed our belongings — a cracked teacup of Mummy's, a battered mug, a bent spoon, some bootlaces, an old sardine tin filled with a pennyworth of salt, a chipped china figurine of a cat, and three slim water-stained books of Father's — into his sleeping sack, and helped me up.

By then, I was so sick, I could not find the

strength to protest. We walked and walked, as he could not quite remember where the convent was. William wanted to carry me, but I stubbornly shrugged him away and kept tottering along. As always, there were other wretched souls wandering the streets, or slumped in odd corners, but they never looked at us.

It must have been near dawn, and I was asleep on my feet, when he stopped one last time.

"Here you go, then," he said, sounding pleased. He settled me down on an icy stone step and wrapped Father's old coat more tightly about my shoulders.

I knew he was going to leave me, and I started crying so hard, I could not speak.

"You *stay* here," he ordered, "until the ladies wake up."

I was able to choke out his name, and William must have been crying, too, because he blinked a good deal and his voice was thick. He wrapped his arms around me, told me I was his best girl, and promised to come back as soon as he could take proper care of me. Then, as the sky faded from black to grey, he handed me a piece of toffee wrapped in sticky paper.

"Make it last until the ladies come outside," he said.

I knew he was about to leave for good, and I tried to get up so I could follow him.

"*Please*, Margaret," he said, tears covering his cheeks. "Do as I tell you." Then he smiled at me — I tried to smile back — and kissed me on the forehead before quickly walking away. He did not wave, or even look back, and I watched him until he disappeared around the corner.

When he was gone, I sobbed until I thought my chest might break apart. It hurt very badly whenever I took a breath, and my whole body shook with each harsh bout of coughing. I was dizzy and hot, and the gas lamps seemed to twirl around me.

Some time later, I heard a horse's hooves clattering on the street, and the sound of a rickety cart trundling along. But I was too weary to look up, or even try to open my swollen eyes.

"'Ere now, wot's all this?" a deep voice said above

me. There was a clank as he set down some milk-cans, then a harsh knocking on the thick wooden door where I was leaning.

The door creaked open, and there were more voices, but I stayed huddled inside Father's coat, still crying. I can remember just staring at the cans of milk. I wanted one *so much*. Weak as I was, I had a notion that I could nick one and dash away before they could stop me. I even reached out a shaking hand, but then thought of how ashamed Mummy would be, and pulled it back.

I could not make sense of what was happening around me, but the man seemed to be gone and the voices were all female now. There was talk of calling a police ambulance, and whether a child who was so ill could be brought in among the others, and then whether, after all, they could do anything *other* than bring in such a child. The last thing I remember is a warm hand on my forehead, and then someone lifted me up and carried me inside the building.

When I awoke, many hours later, I was in a bare white room with a strange, sharp odor. I found out later it was the infirmary. A lady in a big black cape was sitting by the narrow iron bed. Her clothes frightened me, but her face was kind. I remember that she spooned some beef broth into my mouth, and washed my face with cool water from a tin basin.

I have been here ever since.

Monday, 1 April 1912

St. Abernathy's Orphanage for Girls
Whitechapel

Yet again, I cannot seem to fall asleep. So I am writing by moonlight. All day, I have been wondering how long it will take William to receive my letter. How surprised he will be! Postage is a luxury, so as a rule, we only exchange one letter a month. He is working very hard as a bricklayer, somewhere in the city of Boston. He lives in a boardinghouse run by an Irish immigrant lady in Charlestown, which he assures me is almost as fashionable a neighborhood as Whitechapel. The mail can be so slow that it is actually possible I will arrive in the States before he even finds out that I am coming!

Once I get there, I would like to keep going to

school, but I know that will not be possible. I will have to work, to help support us. I am sure that, like London, Boston has factories, and saloons, and rich ladies who need maids — so, I should be able to find a job.

I have not seen my brother since the summer before last, although it seems even longer. He must have grown a great deal by now, as he is almost sixteen. For all I know, he will scarcely recognize me, either.

One of the reasons I miss him so is because I am afraid I have never been one for making friends. Not by design, mind you. Still and all, I have few talents in this area. It may be because I am loath to share my feelings. Also, I read too many books and speak, as I am often told, "like a right toff." My not having the grace to be ashamed of this worsens the situation. Father always said —

Later

I stopped writing for a while, as Nora was crying out in her sleep again. She is so small and alone that I always like to keep a special eye on her. She tends to follow me about a good deal of the time, but I find this to be a compliment, more than anything else, and slow my pace so she can keep up. At supper, she likes me to help her cut up her food, and butter her bread for her. She is an adorable child, and I am happy to do it.

I sat with her for quite some time just now, talking softly so we would not wake the others in the dormitory, and trying to calm away her tears.

"You was down the 'Dilly?" she asked. Nora speaks in the very sweetest and pure Cockney. "And 'ad you Rosy Lee?"

I agreed that I had, indeed, been to Piccadilly, before having a scrumptious tea at the fancy hotel. I had brought her home a few petits fours and some smushed trifle, which she had eaten happily, without leaving the tiniest crumb behind. That only made me wish I had managed to set aside even more for her.

Unfortunately, talking about this reminded her that I would soon be leaving for America, and she began to cry all over again. I promised—as I had several times already in recent days—that I would write her lots of letters and that someday, when we were both rich ladies, maybe we could visit each other. She found this to be scant comfort, so I changed the subject by telling her a very long story about cats, and Buckingham Palace, and *astonishing* amounts of candy. This lulled her to sleep, finally, and now I am back up in my bunk, looking out the window.

There is no question in my mind that Nora and Sister Catherine are what I will miss most about living here. It is several days away, but I already dread our final parting, as I know that the chances of our meeting again are very slight, indeed.

There are few things more difficult in life than saying good-bye to people.

Tuesday, 2 April 1912

St. Abernathy's Orphanage for Girls
Whitechapel

Tonight, the moon is obscured by fog, so I can barely see to write. Not that my handwriting is admirable under the best of conditions.

After William left me here at St. Abernathy's, several months passed before we saw each other again. I wondered endlessly where he was, what he was doing, and how he was surviving on his own. Even *if* he was surviving on his own. Then, one Sunday afternoon, the littlest Murphy sister — there are four of them living here, each more freckled than the next — came to tell me that a young man was waiting to see me in the visiting parlour. At first, I was perplexed, since I do not *know* any young men. Then I was overjoyed, realizing that it could only be my brother.

I ran out of the library so swiftly that Molly Murphy was left quite startled — and Sister Judith even more so, when I dashed slam-bang right into her near the kitchen.

William was standing by the window, looking out at the grey, rainy day. He was wearing a thin black sweater and frayed wool pants, with a cloth cap hanging out of one pocket. It was the first time I had ever *seen* him in long pants. His face and hands were very clean, but his clothes were soot-stained, and he looked so much more grown-up than I remembered. Sister Eulalia was posted right by the door, with an expression of great suspicion on her face. Girls at the orphanage do not—*ever*—receive young men. I assume Sister Mary Gregoria was lurking nearby, also.

"William!" I said happily.

He turned, his whole face changing when he smiled. "Sure, and she's *tall*."

"Sure, and we get *bowls and bowls* of porridge here," I answered.

We both laughed, while Sister Eulalia—who often helps with meal preparations—frowned. I introduced them, and after a few moments, she went out to sit in the hall to give us a bit of time to get caught up.

There was so much to talk about! I have to admit now that I cried a good deal, because it was so wonderful to see him after worrying for so long.

He had brought along a small bag of toffee and licorice, which we shared. I had forgotten I even knew how to smile so broadly. For a time, after we parted, he had miserably continued mud-larking. He tried to find a job at one of the breweries, or the foundry, but was told that he was too young. His luck changed when he ran into one of Father's old mates, Mr. Daniels, on the street one day. Mr. Daniels helped him get work on the Docks and secure cheap lodgings in a sailors' home. The home certainly wasn't fancy, but neither was it a workhouse — or a reformatory — and for that, William was grateful. And so was I.

From then on, he came every Sunday. The weeks passed much more quickly, and easily, for me, knowing I could look forward to his visits. He would always bring a gift of some kind — candy, a newspaper, and one special day, a little bundle of hot chips. I wanted to give him something in return, and Sister Catherine patiently taught me how to knit so I could make him a scarf for his birthday. The final result was amateurish to say the very least, but he accepted it with great enthusiasm.

It was the summer of 1910 when William got a chance to sign on as a cabin boy on a cargo steamer heading to America. He did not want to leave me alone in London, but we decided that he would have many more opportunities to make his way in the States. We planned that I would follow him when I was older — and he had enough money to pay for my fare.

The captain on his steamer was an unpleasant man, and William had a difficult journey. He worked long, hard hours, and was so seasick that he subsisted on nothing more than hard biscuits and water the entire time.

This gives rise to a bothersome notion. What if *I* get seasick, too? That would make me a rather unsatisfactory companion, I fear. Never in my life have I set foot on a boat — or even gone in the water, beyond wading in the Thames. However, I suppose worrying about it will not help matters any. I shall simply have to wait, and see — and eat sparingly the entire time, perhaps.

Well, the morning will come sooner than I would like, so I will stop writing for this evening.

Is there not some tradition of counting sheep in order to become drowsy? I think I just might give it a try. . . .

Wednesday, 3 April 1912

St. Abernathy's Orphanage for Girls
Whitechapel

Today I went back into the City to meet my new employer again. This time, I was allowed to go by myself, although I was given many instructions by the Sisters, and warned to keep the small change they had given me hidden in different pockets, so I would be safe from knaves and thieves. I have a bit of experience with thieves, but am quite certain I have never known a knave — or even seen one from a distance.

The dress I wore was an unflattering cut, and an even worse shade of dull maroon. A postulant who did not do well in the orphanage atmosphere and was transferred to a more traditional convent had left it behind with a bundle of other unfortunate, but "earthly," frocks. I do not remember her, but it was clear from the dimensions of the dress that she had been tall — and not slim. Sister Judith and Sister Catherine performed some necessary surgery with great handfuls of pins, and warned me not to move about freely, if possible.

"But, what if I meet a knave, and must take flight?" I asked.

Their reignited concern about just that dreadful possibility eliminated the chorus of wry chuckles I had anticipated.

So, it was off to Claridge's once again. There might have been a more direct way to go, but I repeated our exact motor bus ride, in order to enjoy another walk through Piccadilly Circus. But I resisted buying any food, as I suspected plenty would await me at the hotel. After all, teatime approached.

I had hoped we would meet in the Foyer, so I could enjoy listening to that quartet again, but Mrs. Carstairs had a footman downstairs awaiting my — slightly late — arrival. He escorted me up to her suite, where our tea was to be served privately. I was concerned that my table manners had not passed muster previously, but then caught sight of two fluttery young women clutching measuring tapes, and pincushions, and the like. I had, of course, forgotten that I was to be fitted with "appropriate garments." Florence was stalking back and forth in front of the two women, letting out a fierce, if squeaky, growl every so often. This was making the women uneasy, to say the least.

"Hello, Florence," I said.

She wagged her tail at me, then resumed her feisty strut.

I could not tell how large the suite was, as so far I had only seen the entry, but it appeared palatial. Mrs. Carstairs came bustling out, looking both more matronly and more unwieldy than I remembered. Judging from her widened eyes when she saw me and ran her eyes up and down my lumpy dress, I was more obviously working class than *she* had remembered.

"Good afternoon, Margie," she said, quite brisk.

Margie? But I greeted her very pleasantly, regardless — and by the proper name, even.

She waved her hand at each of the two pale, jittery ladies in turn. "This is Hortense, and Mabel. Please be most cooperative with them." She turned to the women. "As you can well see, this is a *dire* situation."

I followed them into a sun-splashed sitting room, where a grand tea was spread out on a lace-covered table by the broad, sparkling windows. A man with sparse white hair, but thick grey muttonchop whiskers, was seated at the table, reading a newspaper and clearing his throat every so often.

"Frederick," Mrs. Carstairs said, "this is Margaret Jane Brady, the child who will be accompanying me."

Jane?

Mr. Carstairs noticed us then, and stood up with a militaristic bow. "Yes, yes, so glad to see you," he said, with a patient, but vague, smile.

I was relieved that he did not want to shake hands, or otherwise be demonstrative. "It is a pleasure to meet you, sir," I said, although I was tempted to call him "Guv'nor," just to hear everyone gasp.

"Her clothes are very common, but I think she will do nicely," Mrs. Carstairs said. "Don't you, Frederick?"

Mr. Carstairs nodded heartily, although his gaze was still lingering on his newspaper. "Yes, yes. Lovely, lovely."

"Splendid," I volunteered.

He looked up. "Yes, yes. Splendid."

"I am to have her fitted now," Mrs. Carstairs said.

Right out in the *open*? Were Americans *utter* heathens?

I sensed a spot of alarm coming from Mr. Carstairs's direction as well, but Mrs. Carstairs was already ushering me into a small dressing room, crowded with more fancy clothes than I had ever seen in one place. And, oh, the shoes! So many glossy, impractical shoes.

"Be thorough," Mrs. Carstairs instructed Hortense and Mabel. "When they are finished, Margie, you may join us for tea."

I despise nicknames, but suspected that pointing this out would make no impression whatsoever.

Hortense and Mabel had a great deal of trouble unpinning me from my dress. Although they were shop girls, and certainly not society ladies, my appearance seemed to offend them, and they exchanged more than one wince. I ignored this, except for mimicking one of Florence's snarls once, just to see them flinch.

After they had finally completed their oddly complex measurements, with muttered comments to each other, they undertook the not inconsiderable challenge of *re*-pinning me into my dress.

"Did you pick this out yourself?" one of them — I think it was Mabel — finally asked.

"Yes, quite so," I said. "It fell off the back of the quaintest little lorry in Whitechapel."

They gave each other knowing glances, and regarded me with somewhat more sympathy than before. Once they had finished the pinning and been shown out by a hotel maid, I found I could move even less freely than had previously been the case. Sitting down promised to be a challenge.

However, I was up to the challenge if I could then tuck into that appetizing array on the tea table. My dinner of bread and jam felt like a memory from my distant past.

Mr. Carstairs rose to his feet when I came in, and I sat down as swiftly as possible, a small shower of pins escaping in my wake. Neither of my tea companions commented upon this, although Mrs. Carstairs at least *noticed* — and frowned.

"I very much appreciate everything you are doing for me, Mrs. Carstairs," I said, very politely, "and urge you not to go to too much trouble."

"Yes, well," she said, after the barest pause.

Our conversation was stilted, and Mr. Carstairs did little more than nod or grunt assent occasionally. I found it appalling that he was drinking coffee—but other than that, he seemed like a pleasant, if somewhat stodgy, chap. Both of them fed Florence tempting tidbits at every opportunity, and she took turns sitting in their laps. Once in a while, she visited me as well, and I would present her with a nibble of ham or chicken. She seemed to dislike watercress.

"What a wonderful hotel this is, Mrs. Carstairs," I contributed at one point.

"Obviously I should rather be at the Savoy, but"— she glanced at her husband—"my Frederick prefers it here."

It developed that they had theater tickets that night, and reservations at a restaurant called Romano's, so soon it was time for me to take my leave. Mrs. Carstairs reminded me, again and again, that I was to return on Tuesday morning, packed and ready to go. We would be taking the train to Southampton, and then sail the next day. Each time she went over the plans, I felt shivers of excitement, and fear. Mr. Carstairs said it had been "capital, just capital" to meet me; I agreed; Mrs. Carstairs went over our schedule one last time; and finally, I gave Florence a pat and headed off. Then I paused by the door.

"So, I am to return on — Wednesday evening?" I said, just for fun.

Mrs. Carstairs's face went so pale that I suddenly felt a bit alarmed. But all she said was, "You are a very impudent girl, Margie."

I graciously agreed with this observation — and left.

Thursday, 4 April 1912

St. Abernathy's Orphanage for Girls
Whitechapel

At breakfast today, Bridget Murphy told me I was hoity-toity, sailing off to America with a rich lady. I nodded, and said that I was, indeed, a right swanker, and Sister Eulalia spoke to me sharply about being prideful. I could hardly disagree—but did so anyway out of devilment. Sister Eulalia failed to find any humor in this.

My mind wandered during arithmetic, and I could not even pay attention when we turned to literature. I was thinking about many things, but mainly, I was wondering what it will be like to spend so many days traveling across the sea, surrounded by rich ladies and gentlemen. Apparently, many of them are among the wealthiest people in the world! I hope I will not seem too out of place. Surely my humble station will be obvious to one and all—especially those of English extraction. I hope Sister Catherine is right that one can hardly run into problems by simply keeping one's own counsel, and smiling every so often. I will just always have to remember to think before speaking. I want to be a *credit* to the Sisters, and to the memory of my dear parents, and so will have to rise above my natural tendency to misbehave.

Here in Whitechapel, it is hardly unusual to be

poor. In fact, it is not even *interesting*. But I admit that I still find it hard to understand why most of the girls at the orphanage will be perfectly happy if they get a factory job, marry some nice bloke, and pass the rest of their days within a block or two of here. Most, I think, will be quite content simply to live a life without surprises. I am not sure *what* it is that I want, but I know that it is something more than that which I see every day. I expect to learn a great deal from my journey, and hope I can put it to some good use in my life. The girls would call this cheeky, and I suppose it is. But America is supposed to be the land of endless opportunities, and I see no reason not to try to better myself.

Oh, dear, I believe Sister Eulalia has just caught on that I am writing something of my own, rather than methodically working on my declensions. She looks very indignant, so I believe I will now set this diary aside.

Quickly.

Sunday, 7 April 1912

St. Abernathy's Orphanage for Girls
Whitechapel

This morning, Sister Catherine took me over to the St. Botolph parish for Easter mass. She explained that he is the patron saint of travelers, and she wants to be sure that I leave with his blessings. Our fellow worshipers were a bizarre mix—ranging from prostitutes to the very flagrantly pious—and it was quite different from my normal mass experience. But, because it was Easter, they were all unusually well turned-out. I rather enjoyed it.

On the way home, Sister Catherine stopped at a small shop and bought us two lemonades and some toffee. We sat on an old wooden bench to enjoy our snack, and made almost no conversation. Her face was pensive, and I could tell that she was very sad today.

"We never have favourites, you understand," she said suddenly. "It would not be proper."

I nodded; she nodded; and we sat in the sun and finished our toffee.

It is my last night here, and I suddenly feel quite tearful, sitting up in my usual window. Earlier, I packed a musty old carpetbag Sister Judith found with some underclothing and stockings, a sleeping gown, a brown sweater, my plaid dress, Father's old wool coat, and Mummy's chipped china cat. On further reflection, I took out the cat, for I will give it to Nora, to remember me by. I know Mummy would not mind — and besides, I still have her beautiful silver locket, which I wear night and day, close to my heart. The locket may be somewhat battered and tarnished, but that does not diminish its value to me in any way. I will keep Father's copy of *Hamlet*, but will sign my name under his in the volume of sonnets and present it to Sister Catherine in the morning. I hope she likes it.

I wonder if William has received my letter yet. I suspect not. Still, it would be nice to know that he was expecting me. But I do not think he will mind being surprised, either. And now he will not have to worry about spending the money he has been laboriously saving for my passage.

On the whole, I think Mrs. Carstairs makes me almost as nervous as I make her, so thank goodness for Florence. At least I know I will have *one* friend on the ship. When I get to Boston, I hope William will not mind our getting a cat or two—and maybe a dog as well. I have always wanted to have pets of my own.

At supper tonight, the Sisters brought out a pound cake with white frosting as a farewell celebration, and everyone clapped. Perhaps they are just pleased to see me go. Except, of course, for Nora, who wept. I gave her my share of cake, which helped a little. I also stopped Shirley Hallowell—a nice girl, just turned twelve—in the corridor later and asked her to promise to watch out for Nora after I leave. Shirley was quick to agree, which relieved my guilt a little.

It is hard to believe that by this time tomorrow, I will be in another part of England altogether—and on my way to begin a whole new life!

Tuesday, 9 April 1912

The South Western Hotel
Southampton, England

Here I am, in a lovely hotel room, with *my own bathroom*. I have never experienced such incredible luxury. I just took a long, hot bath, complete with a thick blanket of fragrant soap bubbles. Hot water, as much as I wanted! Then I dried off with a warm, fluffy towel, feeling like the very Queen herself. The pillows on my bed are fat with feathers, and my mattress is as soft as a cloud. Mrs. Carstairs is in the room next door, getting what she described to me as "beauty sleep." I can only imagine that *anyone* who slept on one of these delightful beds would wake up looking beautiful.

Before I left this morning, everyone gave me good wishes at breakfast. For once, I had no appetite at all, and merely sipped some tea. Then, I went back to the dormitory and checked my carpetbag one last time. Sister Judith brought Nora in, and the two of us sat together on her bunk for a time. I gave her Mummy's china cat, and did my best to soothe her tears.

"You goin' down the big ship now?" she asked finally.

I nodded, feeling some tears of my own. I promised to draw her a picture of the *Titanic* and post it right away, so that she could look at it whenever she wanted.

"Draw *you* in the picture," she insisted. "And Florence."

I gave her a big hug, until Sister Judith said that it was time for me to go, since it "wouldn't do" for me to be late. The last thing I saw, when I looked back, was Nora crying and holding the china cat, her feet dangling helplessly over the side of the bed since she is so small. The sight made something inside my chest hurt, and I had to look away.

My farewell to most of the Sisters was quite formal. Sister Mary Gregoria gave me enough money for my motor bus fare, and two pounds "for emergencies." I was very grateful for this, and tucked the money away in a safe pocket.

Then Sister Catherine walked me out to the square, where I would board the motor bus. While we were waiting, she gave me another two pounds, and several shillings. I have no idea how she managed to gather up such a sum, but I was sure it would be disrespectful to refuse to accept it. So I did so, thanking her profusely.

"If you ever need — " She stopped. "Well."

I nodded. Then I took out Father's sonnets and handed the book to her. "Thank you for *everything*," I said. "I have depended on you greatly."

The conductor seemed impatient, and it really was time to go. Off at Claridge's, Mrs. Carstairs was probably impatient, too.

"No favourites," I said.

Sister Catherine smiled. "No. Never."

When the bus pulled away, I stared out the window until she faded from sight. I know that I will always miss her. I must keep a very careful record of my journey so that one day I can share it with her.

I was nearly twenty minutes early when I arrived at the hotel, but Mrs. Carstairs was still very anxious. She surveyed my traveling outfit — the same dark blue dress I had worn the first time we met—and sighed a little. Mr. Carstairs was occupied by his newspaper and coffee, although he nodded pleasantly when he saw me.

There were a great many suitcases and trunks piled up by the door—eight or ten, I should say. My lumpy little carpetbag looked very inferior next to them. Meanwhile, Mrs. Carstairs twittered about, fussing with her hair, checking for misplaced belongings, and otherwise making me feel fidgety. Florence pranced behind her, fully enjoying all of the activity.

"Mr. Carstairs, sir?" I asked hesitantly, when his wife seemed to be occupied for the moment in her dressing room. "How are we going to get all of that luggage onto the motor bus?" More to the point, was *I* supposed to carry it?

He laughed heartily, shook his head, and returned to his newspaper.

As it turned out, a hotel liveryman arrived shortly to cart the many trunks away. We were to be driven to Waterloo Station, and then take the train to Southampton, by the sea. To my amazement, we rode in one big black car, and the *luggage* followed by itself in a second car.

At the railroad station, a slew of porters appeared to whisk the trunks off. Mr. Carstairs arranged for our tickets and went ahead to see if our seats met with his approval. Mrs. Carstairs kept daubing her eyes with a lace handkerchief, and sensing the unhappy possibility of a noisy parting, I elected to take Florence for a pre-trip walk along the platform. I had thought that there would be a large crowd of passengers, but Mr. Carstairs said that no, most people would be on the official Boat Train the next morning.

Mrs. Carstairs was still weeping a little when we pulled out of the station, and she waved Florence's paw at her husband, who was still standing on the platform below. Out of respect, I hid my excitement about leaving London for the first time in my life. Actually, I had never even been on a *train* before, and found its chugs and whistles exhilarating.

It would be too overwhelming to think about whether I would ever return to the city of my birth, so I concentrated on looking out the slightly sooty window. My seat was very comfortable, and I sank back into the blue cushions. The window felt cool against my fingers, and the paneling below it was a dark, polished wood. Worried that I might have smeared the polish, I lightly rubbed the spot I had touched with my sleeve.

To my great surprise, both Mrs. Carstairs and Florence fell asleep almost before we had even left the City. They also both wheezed noticeably.

We were passing small houses now, lined up in neat, redbrick rows. The train seemed to be moving so rapidly that I felt just a bit queasy and was glad to have neglected my breakfast.

Once in a while, we came to a slow, shrieking stop, and the conductor would shout, "Surbiton!" or, "Woking!" or the name of some other hamlet with which I was unfamiliar. "Passengers only, please," he would say. "Step lively!" Then, after a brief idling pause, we would chug on our way again.

Gradually, we left the towns behind, and forged into the countryside. How often I had heard about the great beauty of the English countryside! Now, finally, I was getting an opportunity to see it for myself. Green, rolling fields, spring flowers, and here and there, a quaint cottage or sprawling mansion. The roofs of the cottages seemed to be made of thatch, and I wondered if they would leak in the rain. My grey, cluttered, foggy City seemed a thousand miles away. If we had had the time, I would have loved to spend the day in one of those fields, lying in the grass, with nothing but a book, and perhaps some bread and cheese, to keep me company. I think I would stay there all night, watching the stars and waiting for the moon to rise.

Our journey was only about eighty miles, and all too soon, the conductor was announcing, "Southampton!" Mrs. Carstairs's eyes fluttered open, and she yawned widely.

"What an exhausting trip," she said.

Yes, having a bit of a lie-down *was* always quite a tiring activity.

The conductor helped us off the train, and two red-uniformed porters hurried over to greet us. Once all of the baggage had been collected, they trundled us through a passageway, toward the

South Western Hotel, where we would be staying. I could smell the water, but from where we were, I could scarcely see the *quays*, let alone the ships in the harbour beyond.

We were taken up to the third floor on a sparkling clean lift, although I swallowed hard to think of being wafted off the ground like that, held by thin cables. Still, our ride was steady, and in less than a moment, there we were. It developed that one of the trunks was *mine*, filled with my new "appropriate clothing."

When I opened it to peek inside, I discovered petticoats, stockings, a pair of shiny black shoes, three dresses, a skirt, two high-necked blouses, two hats, and a pink wool coat! *Pink*. I should certainly have chosen another shade, but it was very pretty. One of the hats was decorated with ribbons and flowers, and looked altogether garish. That one, Mrs. Carstairs explained, was to be worn with the green silk dress on fancy occasions aboard the ship. I thanked her, and complimented her impeccable taste. Or had it, perhaps, been Mabel and Hortense's taste? Regardless, looking at these clothes, I felt sadly removed from St. Abernathy's and our faded, patched near-rags.

After an early supper in the hotel dining room — I had the most delicious mutton chops — I took Florence out for a walk. There was still enough daylight for me to explore a little, and I headed directly for the docks. Railroad tracks cut across the street in unexpected places, and I made my way cautiously. Florence found the rumbling of a passing lorry offensive, and barked aggressively at it for quite some time.

Just ahead, there were masts and funnels and metal cranes to be seen in every direction. It was impossible to get a good view of any one ship, as there were so many berthed in the harbour. Also, the railway station and other surrounding buildings obscured my view.

I asked a passing workman which one was the *Titanic*, and he stopped to point her out with great pride.

"There she is, miss," he said, beaming. "Wit' the four funnels. The grandest ship you could ever hope to see!"

I began counting funnels, trying to locate her, but still was not sure that I was looking in the right place. There was a great deal of activity on the quays, and a fair number of gawking passersby, too. Everyone, it seemed, wanted to catch a glimpse of the new ship before her maiden voyage.

Then, all of a sudden, there was a great black hull, stretching farther than my eye could see. I tilted my head back, and the ship loomed above me, looking taller than most of the buildings I have ever seen. Never could I have imagined such a mammoth structure. I noticed now that the train station connected directly to the ship, and that men were loading all sorts of cargo down the gangways, or with towering cranes. There was a feeling of excitement about me, as the workers jostled each other and shouted orders, and onlookers pointed out what little they could see from their various positions.

The *Titanic* was bigger than seemed humanly possible, bright and shiny and smelling of fresh paint. I do not know what I had expected, but the sight of her took my breath away. Florence seemed dismayed by it all, and lay down, resting her head on her forepaws. I patted her, but kept craning my neck in an attempt to take in as much of the ship as I could.

It is hard to believe something so gigantic can float — and yet there she sits, peacefully atop the water. She looks sturdy; she looks *proud*. Were you to pick her up, with a great Godly hand, and drop her in the midst of Whitechapel, I do believe she would smother my entire neighborhood. She was built in Ireland — by fine, strong men like my father and William — and I am filled with admiration at the thought of mere mortals creating something so stupendous.

Florence grew restless, and so, reluctantly, I took her back to the hotel. It would soon be dark anyway.

"I was afraid you had toppled into the water," Mrs. Carstairs said apprehensively, upon my return.

Well, that *would* be unfortunate, as I do not know how to swim. "Florence wanted to linger," I said.

Mrs. Carstairs decided that it would be fun to play cards before bedtime — and was dismayed to find out that I know very few games. She pro-nounced that bridge would simply be out of the question, but quickly taught me how to play hearts. We did this for an hour or so — by which point, I was winning more often than she might have liked. So she told me that it was time to retire, and I did not disagree, as I was eager to come in here and write down my thoughts.

But the hour is very late now, so I believe I will stop for the night.

Wednesday, 10 April 1912
RMS Titanic

So much has happened today that I scarcely know where to begin. The *Titanic* is, to put it bluntly, the most magical and astounding place in the world. Bigger, grander, and more exotic than I could pos-sibly have predicted. She is awe-inspiring, and yet, *comfortable*. Right now, I am sitting in a deck chair on what they call the Promenade. I was up on the Boat Deck for a while, but the wind grew too cold for me, so I moved down to the more enclosed

Promenade. Mrs. Carstairs is off in her cabin, having a rest before supper, and Florence is curled up on my lap, snoring.

I guess I should start with this morning, and our final hours at the South Western Hotel. I had thought I would never be able to fall asleep, but awoke to find sunshine filling my room. A liveryman brought tea and toast right to my room, without my even asking, which pleased me a great deal. I fear that I could grow accustomed to this special treatment! I took another bath — simply because the shiny white tub was *there* — and then put on one of my new dresses. Mrs. Carstairs has made it clear that she does not want to see me in any more "hideous convent discards," and I suspect it is not worth the breath it would take to argue. Anyway, this dress is golden yellow, made of a material I cannot identify, but the cloth feels very soft. The fancy petticoat makes the skirt billow out amusingly. My new shoes seemed slippery against the floor, so I put on my dependable old boots, instead. The dress is long enough so that no one will be able to tell anyway.

I brushed my hair, then pinned it back as well as I could so that it would not fly about. In the trunk, I even found a pair of white gloves, so I wore them, too, just for amusement.

When I appeared at Mrs. Carstairs's door, she squinted through her glasses and then nodded in approval.

"*Much* better," she said, "but do not neglect your hat."

I assured her that I would not dream of doing so, and went back to get the plainer of the two. I dread having to wear the gaudy one, as I am sure I will look quite the imbecile.

We had a most leisurely breakfast. I ordered delicate shirred eggs, along with sausage, kippers, and a jacketed potato. At St. Abernathy's, eggs were always a special treat and you would receive a soft-boiled one only on Christmas, Easter, and your birthday. I was surprised that Mrs. Carstairs, like her husband, preferred coffee to tea, but that must be the way Americans do things. She did not seem to fancy kippers, either. In both cases, I felt that it was a wretched mistake on her part. Florence enjoyed a small plate of chopped ham and the crusts from Mrs. Carstairs's toast. Early on, I spilled a tiny bit of marmalade on my sleeve and quickly blotted it away with a damp napkin, hoping that no one would notice.

Many of the other people in the hotel dining room also appeared to be *Titanic* passengers, as they would look eagerly in the direction of the docks whenever the great steam whistles blasted away. There were even a few children, who sat in their fine clothes much less self-consciously than I did. The boat whistles had been blaring all morning, announcing to all of Southampton that it was Sailing Day. As the town was a bustling seaport, I suspected that they heard these ship whistles on a regular basis, and grew weary of them.

After our meal, it was time to go upstairs and prepare for our leave-taking. Apparently, passengers from the Boat Train were already boarding the ship. Porters arrived with wheeled carts to take our luggage away, and Mrs. Carstairs handed out folded wads of banknotes with a casual air. The porters and bellhops were elated to accept them.

As we crossed Canute Road and approached the quay, it became more difficult to navigate through the crowds. Trunks and bags and overstuffed boxes were piled everywhere, and I wondered how the porters could possibly keep track of them all. People crowded every possible space, and it was hard to separate the passengers from the onlookers. Only the various workingmen, with their confident movements and expressions of tense concentration, stood out to me.

The side of the ship seemed to have openings all over the place, and gangways stretched out to meet them from the railroad platform and the quay itself. The gangways looked rather like wooden bridges, with waist-high railings. Men and women in plain, sensible outfits were boarding on the lower decks, while the gangways above were packed with people arrayed in the grandest fashions. By virtue of clothing alone, it was not at all difficult to tell which passengers were steerage, and which were first class. Presumably, the second-class passengers were the ones boarding somewhere in the middle.

I saw a thin girl in a kerchief and grey wool dress

who seemed to be watching me somewhat enviously from farther down the quay. I realized then, with a start, that my appearance made her think that *I* was a young lady of privilege. The thought struck me funny, and I was tempted to raise my skirt enough to show her my worn old boots. But she was already gone, and I was following Mrs. Carstairs up a flight of stairs towards one of the first-class gangways.

I had never seen such a crowd in my life, and could not quite picture how many of us could fit inside the ship. Enough, I assumed, so that you might never see the same person twice. But I suppose some of the people were only here to see others off—or had only come down to stand nearby and vicariously enjoy the excitement of the day.

Walking across the gangway, I had a moment's unease, wondering if I *really* wanted to get on such a gargantuan ship and float off into the middle of the ocean. Dry land seemed so much more familiar, and safe. In truth, I have never ridden in a dinghy. For that matter, I have never even floated on a *raft*.

"Please do not dawdle, Margie-Jane," Mrs. Carstairs said sharply, as a rather handsome ship's officer waited to greet us at the end of the gangway.

I nodded, and quickened my pace. To my surprise, seen up close, the side of the ship was pieces of metal welded and riveted together. I do not know what I had expected – not wood, obviously – but the bumpy appearance caught me off guard. I guess I thought it would be smooth and seamless, which only goes to show you how little I know about boats. I reached out to touch the metal, finding it – quite predictably – cold and solid. Nearby passengers looked disapprovingly at me, so I yanked my hand away.

We stepped inside the ship into a thickly carpeted hallway. I had not expected carpeting, either. A uniformed man just inside the entry handed us each a small nosegay of flowers from a large wicker basket next to him. No one had ever given me flowers before, so even though it was probably routine on occasions like this, I felt flattered.

From there, we went to the Purser's Office. Mrs. Carstairs handed our tickets and other necessary paperwork to Chief Purser McElroy, and made arrangements to come back later to deposit her valuables in the ship's safe. Once we were back in the corridor, still another smiling dark-haired young man stepped forward. He was wearing a white uniform, and introduced himself as our bedroom steward, Robert Merton. Our staterooms were down on C Deck, and he would be escorting us there, and then be at our service throughout the voyage.

Mrs. Carstairs told him that she had sailed the White Star Line many times before, and began to give him a long list of instructions about exactly when and how she wanted things done. He nodded solemnly at each request, and then smiled at me.

"You would be Mrs. Carstairs's daughter?" he asked, as he led us through a maze of carpeted corridors.

Mrs. Carstairs gasped; I grinned. He might be the first, but he would probably not be the *only* one on the ship who would jump to that mistaken conclusion.

"No, I am her staunch companion," I answered.

"Yes, this is Margaret Jane Brady," Mrs. Carstairs said, recovering her composure. "You may feel free to treat her as you treat me."

Robert nodded, very solemn, although I could see amusement in his eyes.

"You would want to treat Florence just that much *better*," I said, indicating the dog in Mrs. Carstairs's arms.

Robert nodded again, his eyes crinkling at the corners. "That goes without saying, Miss Brady."

So far, I was quite taken by Robert. He looked to be in his late teens, and seemed the sort to be one of William's mates. Mrs. Carstairs ignored this entire exchange, inquiring as to the whereabouts and general safety of her baggage, and whether it would be unpacked for her, or if she would be required to do this herself, a concept she found disagreeable. I was so busy looking around that I missed Robert's answer.

People were milling about, nearly surrounding us, either trying to find their cabins, or exploring the ship and making admiring remarks. I noticed that I was not the only one who could not resist reaching out to touch things. Robert steered us expertly along to a set of three lifts, and we crowded into the first one that opened. Every woman crammed inside seemed to be wearing a different scent, and

I found it a little difficult to breathe through the confusion of strong perfumes. We rode down one deck, and then walked through another corridor. The walls were a pristine white, and the floors still carpeted. It felt as though we were inside a hotel like Claridge's, rather than on a ship. Somehow, I had imagined that a sailing vessel would be much less—substantial.

"You will be right up here, Mrs. Carstairs," Robert said, pointing, "while Miss Brady is just across the way." He opened her stateroom, first, and I could see that our baggage had arrived ahead of us.

There were several boxes of fresh flowers piled up on a low mahogany table near a settee, and Mrs. Carstairs immediately asked to have them arranged in vases at the first possible opportunity. She said proudly that most of them were probably from her dear Frederick, and was he not a thoughtful husband? She also asked that a bowl of fresh water be brought for Florence right away. Robert nodded, and smiled, and nodded some more.

I waited outside in the corridor, watching other patient stewards ushering other demanding passengers to their cabins, each receiving a bewildering litany of instructions and complaints.

"Come knock on my door as soon as you get settled," Mrs. Carstairs said to me. "We will want to be up on the Boat Deck when we cast off."

I nodded, and followed Robert to my stateroom. He had an interesting accent, which I could not quite place. South London, maybe? Manchester? When I asked, he said he was a Liverpudlian — in other words, from Liverpool. Just for fun, I responded with some Cockney, saying that me being a Londoner, that practically made him a "bleetin' fawrner," but still and all, he seemed like a "right stiddy gint who acted proper." He laughed, and instinctively glanced in the direction of Mrs. Carstairs's door to see if she had overheard.

"She has not experienced this side of me yet," I said.

His smile was very broad. "No, I don't suppose she has, Miss Brady."

My stateroom was smaller than Mrs. Carstairs's but still wonderful. Before leaving to tend his other passengers, Robert took a moment to show me where things were — from the washbasin, to the bedside heater, to the button to push for immediate service, and even my life belt, which was resting neatly atop the wardrobe. I would be sharing a lavatory with someone's maid who had the cabin next to mine, but that was certainly not a hardship. He told me to be sure and call him if I needed any help, or even just had a question. Then, with a wink and a slight bow, he left.

I stood in the middle of my cabin, thinking about how lucky I was. I was in my own beautiful room, aboard the RMS *Titanic*, the finest ocean liner in the world, on my way to America!

Later

I was just interrupted in my writing, but it was a pleasure, as a deck steward served me a hot mug of broth. I cannot get over how delightful it is to have people *bring* you things without even being asked. The liquid tastes beefy, and rich, and full of goodness from the marrow. I expect to be quite stout when this voyage is over.

Shortly before noon, Mrs. Carstairs and I went along with the general flow of passengers heading for the upper decks. Florence remained behind, sleeping on Mrs. Carstairs's canopy bed. Instead of taking a lift this time, we climbed what I heard people calling the Grand Staircase. It was, unquestionably, a very impressive piece of architectural artistry—broad mahogany steps winding upward, with a dome-shaped glass skylight above. A statue of a cherub holding a light aloft graced the middle railing, and a beautifully carved wooden clock with a pair of intricately detailed figures dominated the wall at the top of the landing. The time read 11:50.

The railings up on the Boat Deck were so crowded that we could find no place to stand. We moved down to B Deck, and found a small open space along the Promenade. I felt a shiver of excitement each time the steam whistles blew, trumpeting our departure. The air seemed filled with a sense of tremendous anticipation.

Below us, the quay was also jammed by an enthusiastic crowd of people waving their handkerchiefs or hats, and shouting farewells. In return, our passengers were also waving, and tossing single flowers or even full bouquets over the side. Some splashed into the water, while others were caught by lucky onlookers. I am sure I will never be able to forget that feeling of shared festivity and jubilation.

The *Titanic* is such a large ship that a group of tugboats have been assembled to tow us away, out into Southampton Water. As we began to move, ever so slightly, a tremendous cheer rose up. There were other boats berthed nearby, and their passengers and crew members were waving at us, too.

Out of nowhere came several sharp cracking sounds. I was afraid part of the ship had broken apart, but then saw a smaller ship break free of its mooring ropes and veer in our direction. It looked as though she might crash right into us! Some of the people by the railing did not even notice, while others gasped. The *Titanic* did not seem able to turn out of the way in time, but then a wave of water slowed the other ship, and one of the tugboats steered it to safety. An Englishman standing a few feet away from us said, "Well, what can you expect from a ship called the *New York*?" Mrs. Carstairs was not the only

American nearby who did not laugh at this. My fellow Brits, though, were almost uniformly amused.

There was something of a delay as the *New York* was secured, and I heard people grumble about being thrown off schedule. To me, it seemed a minor mishap and hardly worth complaining about. I was merely relieved that an accident had been averted. Two men behind us were talking seriously about the huge wake a ship like the *Titanic* created simply by moving her bulk through the water, and how anything in her path would be helpless in the face of that suction.

As she tends to be so nervous, I would have expected Mrs. Carstairs to be extremely upset about our near-miss, but she was chatting casually with the woman on her left and discussing mutual acquaintances — of which they seemed to have many. We were underway now, but other than a slight sense of engines throbbing somewhere far below me, I could barely feel the ship's motion. Since I had been dreading a constant bobbing and lurching, this smooth and gentle pace came as a relief.

A bugle began trumpeting so close to us that I

jumped. It was being played by a man in a crisp blue uniform with brass buttons. All around me, almost everyone began to move away from the railings and head back inside.

"Come along now, Margie-J.," Mrs. Carstairs said briskly. "Time for our luncheon."

From this, I gathered that it was routine for the sound of a bugle to announce meals. This was far preferable to the forceful banging on tin pots I had heard so many times during my childhood. It is also routine on board to call the midday meal luncheon and the evening meal dinner.

Margie-J. Do all Americans have a penchant for misbegotten nicknames, or is it just Mrs. Carstairs? A vulgar habit, to my way of thinking. Then I heard another American lady up ahead of us happily greeting someone else by shouting, "Bootsie! How *are* you?" Bootsie? God save us from the Colonies.

The first-class dining saloon was on D Deck. We waited, in a crush of people, for a lift, and then rode downstairs. There was a large, inviting reception room in front of us, and a small band was playing off to one side. I did not recognize the tune, but it was very cheery. The reception room was filled with wicker chairs surrounded by small round tables, and an array of large, reedy plants had been placed in strategic locations. It struck me as a cozy place to linger.

The dining saloon itself ran the full width of the ship, and seemed even longer. The room looked as though it could easily serve several hundred people, and yet, the small, elegant tables had, somehow, an intimate feel. The ceilings curved into detailed moldings, and were supported here and there by thin white columns. A plush, patterned carpet covered the floor, and the tall, frosted windows made it seem as though we were anyplace *but* aboard a ship.

It was not my place to take any initiative, so I sat in the chair Mrs. Carstairs indicated. It had a solid feel, with sturdy oaken arms and legs, and medium-green upholstery. At least *two* people my size could have fit in the seat, and I felt rather young and small perched on its edge. If I were not careful, I feared that I might slide right off. It was a chair designed to comfort the corpulent, I suspected.

The tablecloths were white, and a small lamp

with a dark red shade sat in the middle of the table as a centerpiece. A napkin was folded like a pair of wings atop each plate, and accompanied by a daunting array of glassware and cutlery. Sister Catherine had advised me always to mimic whatever the most mannerly person at the table seemed to be doing, and I can only hope that technique will carry me through.

Our table seated six, and shortly we were joined by a Mr. and Mrs. Prescott, whom Mrs. Carstairs was delighted to see. She introduced me in the briefest possible way, and then they were off in an energetic conversation about the spring fashions, the delight of the Russian ballet, and an endless stream of people I did not know, and places I had never been. Even if I had felt bold enough to participate in the conversation, I would have had nothing to contribute to these topics. The Prescotts were pleasant to me, but expressed great disappointment that Mr. Carstairs had been unable to make the voyage. Mrs. Carstairs concurred, and then they began to speak of Broadway and the West End and other theatrical subjects.

Bangers and mash would have done me nicely, but our luncheon was far more impressive than that, with multiple courses. I elected not to drink any wine, and satisfied myself with water, instead. A cold potato soup, salmon, tiny spring peas, crisp asparagus with tart dressing, roasted meats—a stream of black-jacketed waiters bearing silver platters appeared at our table again and again. I generally prefer the heartier taste of mutton, but my sliced lamb was delicious. For that matter, *everything*—right down to the fruit tart and array of cheeses and fruits we were offered for dessert—was delicious.

After our meal, I was ready for a bit of a lie-down myself, so I was pleased when Mrs. Carstairs suggested returning to our cabins. In our absence, her flowers had been arranged, and there was even a bouquet of yellow daffodils in my room! Our clothing had also been unpacked, and the luggage stowed away.

"Fairies came to visit, eh?" I said.

Mrs. Carstairs laughed. "Oh, child, it is quite customary."

An enchanting custom, I should say.

My washstand has been well supplied with thick towels and small scented soaps. After a mite of freshening up, I lay on my bed for a time, marveling once again at how I could scarcely tell that the ship was moving. Even the hum of the engines had begun to seem familiar, and not loud enough to be oppressive.

It was just after three, according to the small clock in my room, when I went to take Florence for a walk, and ultimately ended up here on the Promenade, lounging on a deck chair. Yet another steward even brought me a steamer rug to tuck about my legs so I would not get chilled.

I have been sitting here writing for a while, then pausing to watch people stroll by. A number of children have been playing on the deck, tended by governesses for the most part, as well as the occasional parent. The children have tops, and marbles, and other small toys too numerous to mention. Except for one or two stormy bouts of tears, they all seem to be having a happy afternoon. Part of me would like to go over and join in, but as a hired companion, I do not suppose I am permitted to engage in childish pursuits on this trip. At one point, a ball rolled over in my direction, and I tossed it back to the boy who owned it. Even though he was probably only a year or two younger than I am, he just said, "Thank you, miss," and raced off to continue his game. I cannot help feeling a bit left out — too old to play with the children, and too young and naive to interact with the adults. In these fancy clothes, I can pass for one of them — but, to me, the differences in our social backgrounds feel too huge to overcome.

I suppose I should have a driving desire to examine the ship from top to bottom, but so far, I would rather adjust gradually to being here. There will be plenty of time for exploration in the days to come.

But now I think Florence could do with stretching her small legs, so I will write more later.

Thursday, 11 April 1912
RMS Titanic

I had every intention of continuing my entry last night, but fell asleep almost before I had a chance to lie down. The sea air can do that, Mrs. Carstairs tells me.

We stopped in Cherbourg, France, last night, and more passengers boarded the ship. The water was not deep enough for us to steam all the way in, so smaller boats brought the passengers out and transferred them aboard. "Tenders," those boats are called; I am not sure why. I would like now to be able to claim that I have been to France, but sitting quite some distance offshore does not really count, I suppose. I saw the coast, at least.

This morning, we are en route to Queenstown, Ireland. I hope that we dock close enough to be able to see the land of my father's birth. It would be even better if we were able to disembark, so I could touch the soil of my ancestors, but that seems doubtful.

Robert knocked on my door early this morning, and then brought in tea, scones, marmalade, and a perfect little bunch of grapes. He stayed to talk for a few moments, and I found out that this is his first job as a full-fledged steward, as opposed to being an assistant, and that he was very excited to have been assigned to first class.

"A strange thing happened yesterday," I told him, indicating the cheerful vase on my bedside table. "*Elves* came, and brought me a gift."

"They must have liked your smile, Miss Brady," he said, with a grin. Then, a bell rang in a stateroom somewhere down the hall, and he had to leave to answer it.

I ate every bite of the food he had brought, yet still had no trouble eating a full breakfast in the dining saloon later. Perhaps the sea air makes one hungry, too? Not that having a large appetite is unusual for me, mind you.

After breakfast, Mrs. Carstairs thought it would be nice to spend an hour or two in the first-class writing room, which is next to the lounge. Queenstown will be our last opportunity to post letters before we arrive in New York. Quite a few other passengers seemed to have the same idea, but we were able to find an empty desk and two chairs without much difficulty. There are lots of postcards and fancy vellum stationery available for the passengers to use. The top of the stationery has the same red flag with the White Star logo that I have seen on so many other items, like menus and matchbooks, on the ship. Next to the logo is printed: ON BOARD R M S "TITANIC." I am tempted to slip a few sheets into this diary to keep as a souvenir; I wonder if anyone would mind my doing so. I will ask Robert, maybe, later, if it would be all right. I am hoping that he and I will be friends, as I do not feel at all shy talking to him.

I wrote fairly detailed letters about the trip to William and Sister Catherine, and then worked on a simpler note to Nora. She cannot yet read, but I printed neatly in the hope that she might enjoy practicing. Then I wasted several sheets of the stationery trying to draw an accurate picture of the ship for her to hang by her bed. I began to get frustrated at my lack of even minimal artistic competence, and crumpled one of the sheets so loudly that several people in the room looked up. Mrs. Carstairs was mortified by this unexpected attention, which I attempted to divert by looking around as though I, too, were searching for the dastardly crumpling culprit.

A broad-shouldered man with kind, clean-shaven features stopped next to our desk. I had noticed him walking around, seemingly observing everyone for about twenty minutes, and he must have noticed my sketching struggles. He leaned over and examined my discarded drawings before I had time to cover them with my hand. My face felt hot with embarrassment, as they truly were inept.

"Please excuse my disruption," I said. "I am trying to send a picture to a little girl of whom I am terribly fond."

He smiled, and said he would be happy to put together a quick diagram *for* me, if I would like. I thanked him, but explained that to Nora, *my* having drawn the ship myself would mean more to her than the quality of the rendering.

"Ah," he said. "Well, in that case, may I suggest that you angle the funnels more? Then just try for very clean lines. Long strokes, instead of attempting so much detail."

I gave that a try, and my next effort showed some small improvement.

"There you go," he said. "I think you'll do very nicely now."

I thanked him again, and then he said, "Good day, ladies," and went on his way.

"My goodness, that was Mr. Andrews!" Mrs. Carstairs said in an awed voice, once he was gone.

"A nice fellow," I agreed, drawing intently.

"He *designed* the ship," she said.

Startled, I stopped drawing. "Then I guess he would have done quite an accurate illustration," I said finally.

Mrs. Carstairs shook her head, seeming exasperated. "You are a most curious child, M. J."

M. J. "I thank you, Mrs. Upstairs," I said.

"A very *difficult* child," she said, sounding much more exasperated.

I nodded, sadly, and we both returned to our letters.

Later

I am in my stateroom now, getting ready for bed. Once our letters were completed this morning, we went up to the Boat Deck to watch for Ireland. Mrs. Carstairs did not see the urgency of this, but elected to humour me and come along. The sky was bright blue, and nearly cloudless; the sea, flowing in smooth, dark swells. There was an invigorating breeze, and I took several deep breaths of the wintry air.

Mrs. Carstairs looked uneasy. "Where is your coat, I ask you?"

I assured her that I was quite warm, with my sweater thrown over my shoulders. It is not a fashionable garment, so I knew she would prefer that I not put it all the way on.

How jarring it was to look in every direction, and see nothing but the ocean. Given the implications of that, too much thought would have made me apprehensive, so I decided it would be far better to praise this phenomenon.

"'Oh ye! who have your eyeballs vexed and tired,/ Feast them upon the wideness of the Sea,'" I said.

"Browning again?" Mrs. Carstairs asked, after a pause.

I had only meant to be jovial, not put her in an uncomfortable position. "Keats," I said, after a pause of my own.

She nodded heartily. "But of course."

From now on, I think I will refrain from spontaneous quotations.

The wind was increasing, and more and more people on the deck were retreating to the warmth of the Promenade or one of the public rooms. Shortly thereafter, Mrs. Carstairs decided that she, too, would prefer to go back inside. I promised to join her when the bugler announced luncheon. We were going to try the Café Parisien this time, instead of the dining saloon.

As she left, I observed that I *was* cold, so I gave up and shrugged into my sweater, watching the horizon intently the entire time. If Ireland appeared, I did not want to miss anything. Then I saw grey shapes rising up out of nowhere. Hills? Mountains? As we drew closer, the land grew more distinct. There were steep, stark cliffs, grey and barren, with extraordinary green pastures and hills behind them. The land was both rocky and lush, and I fell in love with it at once. It lacked the civility and dignity of the English countryside, but somehow had a wild, bewitching charm. An intoxicating charm. So much green! How could potatoes ever have *dreamed* of refusing to thrive in fields like that? It seemed a crime against nature, as well as humanity.

Once again, we did not enter the harbour; but, rather, tenders crowded with new passengers rode out to meet us. Realizing that I was looking at Cork, where my father had been born, brought tears to my eyes. How I would have loved to have him standing here next to me, at this very moment. Mummy never got a chance to see Ireland, either, and I know she would be staring as eagerly as I was.

There were other boats following the tenders, with people inside clamoring to come aboard. I asked a bundled-up woman reading in a deck chair what they were, and she said that the boats contained merchants hoping to come aboard and make a quick profit. A few actually were allowed to set up shop while we were anchored, and I heard later that they were displaying the most beautiful lace, along with china and linen.

It was with deep regret that I went inside for luncheon, and I barely noticed my food, so eager was I to return to the Boat Deck and admire Ireland. Two shrill middle-aged sisters were seated at our table, and they told us, at giggling length, about the horrifying thing they had seen while they were out on the deck. A demonlike face had appeared to them, peeking out of the aft funnel, and laughing, as one of them put it, like "Beelzebub himself!" Mr. Prescott, who was also at our table with his wife, assured them that it had certainly been a member of the crew doing maintenance work. The sisters remained convinced that there must be a more sinister explanation. This was altogether too eccentric for me, and I asked to be excused, so that I could go back outside. Mrs. Carstairs agreed reluctantly, but urged me to stay away from the funnel in question, just in case.

Back on the Boat Deck, I was pleased to discover that we were sailing along the coast, rather than heading straight out to sea. A great flock of screeching seagulls was following us, swooping, and diving, and otherwise enjoying the day. I leaned on the railing until well past teatime, watching the beautiful scenery pass by. We passed islands, and lighthouses, and austere, craggy cliffs. The rock formations were fascinating in their variety, and I do not think I could ever get tired of those glorious shades of green in the landscape beyond. Of course, I will always love London, but my father must never have stopped regretting leaving this splendid country behind.

Someday, I must come back to Ireland and see all of that beauty up close.

After dinner tonight—the meal as lavish as ever, I might add—we went up to A Deck to listen to a concert by the five-man orchestra. I was not familiar with many of the tunes, but they were all gay and cheerful, and it was an enjoyable evening. People applauded each effort enthusiastically, and sometimes shouted out requests. The band would respond right away, never once stymied. I found the ragtime particularly engaging. Mrs. Carstairs says it is very popular in the States, and was pleased to answer the many questions I had about American music in general.

I realize that I have yet to do my stateroom justice on paper. Right now, I am reclining on my bed, which has thick blue curtains I can draw around it for privacy, if I so choose. My entire room has been decorated in shades of blue, from the flocked wallpaper to the bedspread to the thick carpet. I even have my own writing desk and dressing table, the latter with a large antique mirror mounted above it. There is also a small sitting area, with a shiny square table and two comfortable armchairs. I have a bedside heater, as well as a ceiling fan. My washstand — with two sinks! — is against the far wall. The paneling is a glossy dark chestnut shade that matches the wardrobe exactly.

I have the porthole opened slightly, to get the air. It is dark, so there is nothing to see, but the breeze is welcome. Otherwise, it feels a little stuffy to me. There are numerous small lamps on the walls and tables, but I like keeping the room somewhat dim and mysterious.

Someone is knocking on my door — I wonder why? I have only just returned from walking Florence, so surely it is not Mrs. Carstairs telling me she needs to go again.

It was Robert, with hot chocolate, some biscuits, and a bright red apple.

"I thought you might want a snack before retiring, Miss Brady," he said. "Most of my passengers do."

I realized that a snack would, in fact, be a welcome treat. "Thank you very much for thinking of me," I said. "It should never have occurred to me to bother you."

His eyes twinkled. "I must say, you are not my most difficult passenger, Miss Brady."

I imagined not, since I heard bells in all of the nearby cabins summoning him constantly. "I would be very pleased if you would call me Margaret," I said.

He hesitated. "We are supposed to treat our passengers with the utmost respect at all times."

"I will keep your disgraceful breach of protocol to myself," I said.

He laughed, and then looked a little tired as two bells chimed simultaneously out in the corridor. "I must bid you good night then, Margaret," he said, and left the room, still smiling.

I finished every bite of the apple and all three biscuits, making my hot chocolate last the entire time. While I ate, I read the Henry James novel I had borrowed from the ship's huge library after breakfast this morning. I also have some Ralph Waldo Emerson essays, and a collection of Emily Dickinson poems, waiting by my bed.

Frankly, I *never* want to leave this ship; it is the most wonderful place on Earth.

Friday, 12 April 1912
RMS Titanic
Somewhere at Sea

I have now discovered that when one is aboard ship, there is a whole new vocabulary to learn. I got Robert to explain some of it to me this morning, when he arrived with tea, toast, and jam. "Port" is left, and "starboard" is right. I think. It is hard to keep all of these new words straight in my mind. The "bow" is in the front of the ship, and the "stern" is in the rear. When people say "amidships," they seem to mean the middle. "Aft" is someplace behind you. Corridors are "alleyways," the kitchen is a "galley," and walls are "bulkheads." And *never*, ever, *ever* would you call the *Titanic* a "boat." She is a "ship." Why ships are called "she," rather than "he," has not yet been satisfactorily explained to me. Tradition, perhaps.

Mrs. Carstairs has found a group of avid bridge players, and they spent most of today playing in the lounge. I watched for a while, but found the intricacies of the game quite dreary.

With Mrs. Carstairs thusly occupied, I had plenty of time to explore today. Her only firm request was that I be certain to come to her stateroom before meals to help her dress. That sounds foolish, but with all of her corsets and petticoats and elaborate dresses, she seems to need an extra pair of hands. She changes before every single meal, and I have yet to see her wear the same outfit twice. This variety seems to be very important to the women on the ship, although for the life of me, I am not sure why. It seems a great waste of time to worry so about fashion. I even grow impatient during the time it takes to comb my hair. Mrs. Carstairs is disturbed that a young *man* is serving as our cabin steward, and says she is tempted to request a *stewardess*, instead. I quickly promised that she could depend on me to assist in any way she desires, and reminded her of the lovely job Robert had done arranging her flowers. She seemed dubious, but finally nodded reluctantly and waved me away.

I went all the way down (G Deck? F Deck? I lost

count) to the swimming pool and squash court this morning, and peeked inside the rooms. I had no urge to engage in either of these activities, but it was entertaining to watch others do so. Later, I examined the Turkish baths, the postal office, and the first-class maids' and valets' dining saloon. I have not run across many of the maids and valets, and rarely even see the young woman who shares my lavatory. Her name is Josephine, and her employer is a crotchety and demanding elderly woman who keeps her so busy that she scarcely has a moment to herself. I am fortunate that Mrs. Carstairs is far more reasonable about such things. We are, perhaps, not an ideal pair, but even my brief glimpses of Josephine's harried face rushing by make me count my blessings.

For amusement, I rode the lifts for a while, and had a nice chat with a boy named Stephen who operates one of them. He is from Southampton, and overjoyed to have found employment on such a fine ship. It is funny—I am really only comfortable here when I am speaking to members of the crew. I am sure I would also feel at ease if I were traveling in steerage, since I would no longer feel like such a fraud. I know how lucky I am, but still, it would have been nice if I had *earned* my passage on this ship.

Later on, I wandered into the gymnasium, and the very fit Mr. McCawley, who oversees the room, demonstrated the various machines for me. In the East End, people are too busy working to *exercise*, but it seems to be different for the leisure class. I did not care for the mechanical horse or camel—far too jouncy and erratic—but I pedaled quite effectively on a stationary bicycle. It is queer to ride and ride and not go anywhere, but there is a clock on the wall with small pointers that move to show how far you have traveled. I also tried the rowing machine, but did not find myself to be very adept at this.

First-class passengers can go anywhere they choose, but the second-class and most especially the third-class passengers are restricted to certain parts of the ship. There are actually locked gates and other barriers to keep the steerage passengers segregated from everyone else. The only time I have seen anyone from steerage is from the end of the Promenade, looking down at the deck by the ship's stern. That particular deck is known — here I share some more of my new vernacular, courtesy of Robert — as the "poop deck." There is almost always a great laughing crowd gathered there, and some man keeps playing the bagpipes. I have also heard a fiddler. It reminds me, fondly, of Whitechapel. First-class passengers tend to frown down at the steerage passengers, pointing and making comments as though they were at the zoological gardens in Regent's Park. This makes me so uncomfortable that I have decided I will stay to the bow end of the ship as much as possible.

I have no sense of what the conditions are like down in steerage, and hope it is not too dreadful. William's stories of *his* transatlantic voyage were horrid — and haunting. I have little sense of what is happening anywhere *other* than the first-class areas. Part of me would like to go down and see steerage for myself, but the idea of being able to pass through the locked gates at will, while others cannot, is terribly offensive to me. I think it would be very contemptuous. In the lift, Stephen told me that a number of first-class passengers have done just that, laughing when they returned and talking about how much fun it was to go "slumming." So, despite my curiosity, I have no intention of doing that myself.

The ship is so big that you can actually get *tired* walking around it. When I bring Florence, I always have to carry her part of the way. She can be fierce, but she is not very hardy. Because it is so cold, Mrs. Carstairs has been making me put a tiny hand-made sweater on Florence before taking her out. This seems whimsical to me, but I am not about to argue. Besides, Florence enjoys preening.

On more than one occasion, I have passed a remarkably tall, mustached man walking his Airedale on the Boat Deck. He has been pointed out to me as Colonel Astor, and Mrs. Carstairs says that he is one of the richest men in the entire world. He never seems to look cheerful, except when he is walking his dog. People are always gossiping about his wife, because she is much younger than he is and, "in the family way." There is so much gossip during meals — about everyone and everything — that I am very glad to be such an anonymous figure. Once people find out that I am only a companion, most of them promptly lose interest in me, and begin to talk to someone else. I am not easily offended, so this bothers me not a twit. Besides, the marvelous meals themselves continue to offer me plenty of distraction.

A man named Mr. Hollings has attached himself to us because we are unescorted. Apparently, gentlemen aboard ship feel a duty to look after women traveling alone. Mrs. Carstairs says her Frederick would be very pleased to know that we are so well protected. His guardianship seems mostly demonstrated by his taking Mrs. Carstairs by one elbow and leading us to our table at mealtimes. If Mrs. Carstairs is out on the deck—a fairly rare event, as she continues to be occupied by marathon card games—Mr. Hollings makes certain that the ever-responsive stewards are paying her what he feels is sufficient attention. Often now, during meals, he joins us, along with a rather weedy young man named Ralph Kittery, whose sole pursuits appear to be polo and the American stock market. Mrs.

Carstairs is much better about feigning interest in these subjects than I am. I can manage nothing better than a vague, impersonal smile, and maybe a nod or two.

What an unusual situation, to be seated at tables full of Americans, meal after meal. They are lively people, but almost childishly gullible. Any Englishman or woman would instantly see through my accent, which is, at best, of the light Oxford variety. I have been introduced to some of the British passengers, in the Reception Room before dinner and so forth, and once I speak, they almost always give me a smile that looks more like a wry wink. But the Americans all seem to think that I sound terribly clever. When I *do* speak, Mrs. Carstairs appears to hold her breath. I am not exactly sure what she fears I will say, but it seems as good a reason as any to remain reserved.

A Mrs. Janson from Philadelphia was included in our dinner group this evening. She is blond and willowy and prone to blinking constantly. She asked where I was from, and when I said Whitechapel, by way of Wapping, she commented upon the beauty of the names. Insofar as Whitechapel is concerned, I wanted to say that yes, Jack the Ripper had apparently shared her affection for this area—but I held my tongue. Rarely do these Americans seem to enjoy my humor. But sometimes, I admit, I cannot resist.

"I met the most remarkable Parisian child on the Boat Deck today," I remarked, during a lull in the conversation tonight. "Scarcely four years old, and already speaking French!"

A puzzled silence fell over the table. Then, to my surprise, Horace, the wine steward, laughed. He was not joined by anyone else, quickly changed the laugh into a cough, and began to refill everyone's glasses.

In the meantime, I returned to my haddock. And soon, the conversation shifted, once again, to the many joys of the summer season in Newport.

Such are the social interactions I have been experiencing. I must be a terrible disappointment as a companion, since Mrs. Carstairs and I are able to find little common conversational ground. But I am continuing to assume a number of mundane housekeeping chores for her, so I guess I am fulfilling the requirements of a maid. These tasks include sending her clothes out daily to be sponged and pressed, changing the water in her flower vases, ordering trays for her, and of course, taking very good care of Florence. Devoted as Mrs. Carstairs is to her dog, she does not seem to enjoy walking her — or, more crucially, cleaning up after her. Yesterday, Florence caught me off guard right at the end of a row of covered lifeboats, and a passing ship's officer gallantly contributed his handkerchief to the cause.

I was happy to retire somewhat earlier than usual tonight; my day of exploring fatigued me. The sound of those steadily throbbing engines below is very soothing, and also helps lull one to sleep. With all of the many sights on the ship, I still think that I like the reading and writing room best of all. I could easily spend the full day there, and never grow restless.

Between that room, and the library, I would have no trouble finding activities to amuse myself.

The weather was so lovely today. I hope tomorrow is just as nice!

Saturday, 13 April 1912

RMS Titanic

I really enjoy the morning ritual of having tea and scones in my room — and as much conversation as we can manage before the peal of a bell calls Robert away. He has taken to bringing an extra scone or two, and joining me in my meal.

"How is it down in steerage?" I asked him today.

"Oh, quite comfortable," he assured me. "I would be right pleased to journey that way myself. I've seen ships where *second* class is not so nice as our third."

I gave that some thought. "How are *your* cabins, then?"

"Well, we have very little time to spend there," he said, after a pause. "And it was a great piece of luck, my catching on with this crew. Many's the week I could find no work, and my mum sore needs the money."

"My brother made his passage as a cabin boy on a fair rotter of a steamer," I said. "I never thought I would be anywhere *but* steerage."

He winked at me. "So, we've both had a bit of luck, then."

As always, bells began to chime, and he was off. Each morning, he includes the *Titanic*'s small newspaper on my tray, the *Atlantic Daily Bulletin*, and I picked it up to read. The stories are more chatty than informational, and report items such as the number of miles we have cruised during any given twenty-four-hour period. As the weather has been no handicap, the ship seems to do better and better, and there is a daily contest for passengers to predict the actual figure. We are expected to arrive in New York on Wednesday morning. Oh, I hope William is standing there on the dock waiting for me!

Later

This afternoon while I was on the starboard-side Promenade, Colonel Astor stopped to pat and admire Florence. He had his own dog in tow, and I asked him what the dog's name was. When he said, "Kitty," I laughed, which clearly pleased him. He may be an imposing figure, but how could you dislike a man who named his dog "Kitty"?

Mrs. Carstairs and I took tea in the Café Parisien, instead of the lounge. The atmosphere is much less formal than the dining saloon, and we had a harmonious time. There is a light, airy feel to the room, complemented by numerous plants and wicker chairs. Trains of ivy actually climb the walls! We were joined by several other ladies, one of whom had a great booming laugh, which she employed regularly. Her name is Mrs. Brown, and people seem to think her amusing, but boorish. Since she sat down right next to me, and plied me with friendly questions, I liked her at once. If anything, discovering that I was a mere companion only increased her attention. She feels that I will find America smashing, and that Boston will suit me well, as the area is famous for its educational institutions. I was encouraged by this information, and hope that her predictions are accurate.

For some reason, Mrs. Carstairs is tired of bridge today, so I played hearts with her — still the only game I know — until it was time to help her dress for dinner. She instructed me to wear my paisley dress, and to save the green silk for tomorrow. I did as I was told, and she surveyed me critically before asking me to take off what she described as "that dreadful locket." This stung me, but I only said mildly that it had belonged to my beloved mother and there were no circumstances under which I would ever take it off. *None* whatsoever.

"All right, then," she said, studying my neckline, and finally sighed. "I will lend you a scarf."

It was not until we were waiting for a lift that she remembered to apologize for offending my mother's memory. I accepted this graciously, but touched the locket protectively. All it contains are tiny dark locks of hair from when William and I were babies — I should rather have photographs of my parents — but I treasure it, regardless.

We were heading for the à la carte restaurant, which everyone calls "The Ritz," after a famous hotel. I may not appreciate the connection, but I am sure there is one. "The Ritz" is smaller, and more elegant than the dining saloon. The chairs are upholstered in a floral pattern, and the groupings are less linear. The walls are paneled with an almost golden shade of wood, and there are many inset mirrors. Mr. Hollings, who is dining with us again, says that the mirrors give the room the illusion of space. I took him at his word.

Our napkins had been folded into upright cones, and the gold-rimmed china is an entirely different pattern from the dishes I have seen elsewhere on the ship. I feel sorry for the people who have to wash all of them!

I have studied French, but not sufficiently enough to translate the menu with confidence. It is possible to order a full nine courses, but even my appetite is not quite equal to that task. I tried caviar for the first time — and do not expect to repeat the experience. Very salty, very strongly flavored, and the eggs had a slippery feel I found unappetizing. I seemed to be the only one at the table to have this reaction, as the caviar disappeared twice as fast as the plover's eggs and other appetizers.

With each course, we are served a different wine. I sip some of the glasses, but have yet to come close to finishing one. When the waiter offered to bring me some lemonade, I accepted eagerly.

After the meal, I was glad to have the excuse of needing to walk Florence, as I felt quite overstuffed. How do ladies like Mrs. Carstairs manage to eat *at all* while laced into those corsets? I count myself lucky that I have never been forced to put on such a restrictive garment. I suppose it will be inevitable when I am a little older, but I hope to put that particular symbol of maturity off as long as possible.

Florence and I each wore our sweaters, as it was cold on the Boat Deck. I sat in a deck chair for a few moments, breathing the refreshing air and looking up at the stars. In every other direction, I could only see the blackness of the ocean. Mostly, I could not even see *that*, but I sensed it. The ship's lights seem warm and comforting in the midst of this lonely ocean.

A first-class gentleman — I do not remember his name — walked past me, and began to light a cigarette.

"Excuse me, miss," he began — and then paused to look at me more closely. "Aren't you Evelyn Carstairs's maid? I am not sure you are permitted out on this deck."

I instantly felt ashamed, but also angry. "I am chaperoning the dog," I answered.

He shrugged, lit his cigarette — right in front of me! — and continued on his way. Gentlemen *never* smoke in front of ladies — but I guess servants do not count.

My peaceful time ruined, I got up and returned inside. I must try to remember that, for the most part, people on the ship have been very nice to me, indeed. And he had smelled of whiskey, so perhaps he was not in his right mind.

Even so, it hurt my feelings.

Sunday, 14 April 1912
RMS Titanic

This morning, we went to a religious service in the dining saloon. I took great solace from this, which suggests that I may be more devout than I would have estimated. At St. Abernathy's, we attended some form of mass every day, and it became part of the fabric of my life. The sight of nuns and priests came to be a comforting one to me. This mass was being called a Divine Service, presumably so that passengers of every faith would feel comfortable attending. Second- and third-class passengers were welcome, but not as many took advantage of this as I would have thought. Many of the ones who did come took unobtrusive seats, or stood, in the back of the crowded room. I was very tempted to join them, but knew that it would upset Mrs. Carstairs, and so I just stayed where I was.

Rather than a clergyman or priest, the service was led by Captain E. J. Smith himself. I know he is very busy commanding the ship, but he also mingles in passenger areas sometimes. He has a formidable appearance, with his dense grey beard and solemn eyes, but his voice is soft and almost melodic. Everywhere he goes, people want him to stop and talk to them, and he seems to be unfailingly polite. Mrs. Carstairs is somewhat miffed that we have yet to dine at his table, although today we are to have lunch with the Purser, Mr. McElroy, and the affable ship's doctor, Dr. O'Loughlin. She feels certain that if her Frederick were here, her social standing would rise considerably.

At the service, we were each handed a copy of the White Star Line's Book of Prayer. Many of the prayers and psalms were familiar, while others had a specific nautical theme. The orchestra accompanied us on all of the hymns, which culminated with a rousing chorus of "O God, Our Help in Ages Past."

At one o'clock, the bugler called us to luncheon. At St. Abernathy's, bells summoned us throughout the day; now, I respond to a bugle. This may or may not be progress.

As we are going to be at a more prestigious table than usual, Mrs. Carstairs told me to change into my yellow dress and to take extra care with my hair.

Most of our mealtime conversation concerned an endless stream of questions directed towards Purser McElroy and Dr. O'Loughlin. As senior members of the crew, it is expected that they are privy to special snippets of inside information. There was much talk about the ship's performance, and whether the rumor that we might reach New York on Tuesday night, rather than the following morning, is true. One gentleman at our table — I forget his name — even wanted to know if the tales of icebergs ahead were reliable. Most of these questions were dodged with vague generalities. So my tablemates moved on to compliments, and complaints about many of the ship's amenities. These, Purser McElroy addressed with more authority.

I, of course, concentrated on savoring my meal, since I was ravenous. It would not have been appropriate to eat before the Divine Service, so I had declined breakfast this morning. I had been afraid that this would offend Robert, but he said he was only too pleased to respect my wishes. I *did* sip some tea, and we talked a little about what it had been like for him growing up with five sisters and three brothers in Liverpool. It sounded as though he had been raised in a close and jolly family, even though he said that he and his brothers had gotten into "many a scrap." I admitted that while I preferred only to remember the happy times, William and I had been known to have a row or two ourselves. A row or *three*, William probably would have said.

During my third course, Dr. O'Loughlin smiled across the table at me. He has white hair, and seems terribly kind. "You do not suffer from a delicate constitution, do you, child?"

"I embrace culinary excess, sir," I said, and he laughed.

"Spoken like a true Edwardian!" Purser McElroy proclaimed, and more people chuckled.

After that wonderful feast, I was content to read in my room, while Mrs. Carstairs napped. Before it was time to dress for dinner, we went to the Purser's Office, so that she could retrieve some of her jewels. Then we stopped by the wireless office, so that she could send a telegram to her son-in-law, to let him know that she might arrive earlier than expected. The two young men working in the Marconi room were strikingly civil, but I saw a huge stack of messages piled in two baskets, and they seemed somewhat overwhelmed.

That evening, it took Mrs. Carstairs much longer than usual to get ready. She wanted me to help her arrange a singularly fancy hairdo, but my efforts on her behalf were clumsy. In the end, she summoned a friend's maid to assist her, all the while directing me to watch *very closely* so that I would be able to do it myself next time. I suspected that she was over-dressed, but soon discovered that elaborate evening gowns with an abundance of accessories were the norm tonight. The men wore black dinner jackets and looked very debonair, indeed.

I was a little unsteady in my new shoes, but put them on to make Mrs. Carstairs happy. My green silk dress felt very sleek, and I carefully pinned my ornate, gaudy hat to my hair. It rested at a tilt that seemed jaunty to me, so I did not adjust it. Mrs. Carstairs also gave me an extra pair of her gloves, which reached almost all the way to my elbows!

Anyone who had accused me of being hoity-toity at this particular moment would have been absolutely correct.

When we walked into the Reception Room for pre-dinner cocktails, the sight of my fellow passengers decked out in their very best was impressive. Trains and bustles, stylish jackets and stoles, furs and pearls, lace and satin, gold and emeralds, each hat more decorative and festive than the last. Tonight is an extra-special occasion as people will be concentrating on their packing tomorrow.

Mr. Hollings fetched Mrs. Carstairs a glass of wine, and me some mineral water. When it was time to go in for dinner, his stodgy young friend, Mr. Kittery, glanced over, looked again, and then offered his elbow to me. This gave me the sense that my appearance — or at least the quality of my silk dress — was moderately successful tonight. Mrs. Carstairs reminded him, sharply, that I am only a young girl, and he should behave in a gentlemanly manner. Since all he wanted to do was share yet another series of tales about his many polo exploits, I think her concern was misplaced.

Everyone in the dining saloon seemed to be in high spirits, and animated conversations raised the usual noise level. I tried a raw oyster for an appetizer, and found its salty intensity a bit much. The next course of cream of barley soup was more to my liking. No sooner had I laid down my spoon or fork than my plate was swiftly taken away and replaced by a fresh one.

The stream of silver platters borne by restaurant stewards came at a steady pace. Among other treats, I enjoyed roast duckling, château potatoes,

and creamed carrots. For dessert I selected a chocolate éclair with vanilla ice cream. By now, I was quite
satiated, and saw no need to avail myself of the traditional cheese-and-fruit course.

After a repast like that, it was almost surprising
that any of us were able to *walk*. Some of the passengers seemed rather tipsy, but it was all in the spirit
of celebration and good fun. Tonight's concert by
the orchestra was even more stirring than usual,
and I sipped a raspberry cordial throughout.

It has become so cold that I took Mrs. Carstairs's
advice and wore my pink coat when I walked
Florence. It may have clashed with my gown, but
there were very few people outside to notice. As a
rule, there are many affectionate couples strolling
about, but tonight, the frigid temperature seemed
to have dissuaded most of them, and I often had full
stretches of deck to myself. Fortunately, there was
no sign of the rude gentleman with the cigarettes.

The sky was so astoundingly clear that I stopped
and gazed up in outright fascination. The ocean
was so smooth that it looked like glass, and the
stars had an incomparable brilliance. The moon

had yet to rise, but the starlight more than compensated for this. What an extraordinary evening it had been!

Once Florence was safely situated back with Mrs. Carstairs, I treated myself to a comfortable soak in the tub and changed into my sleeping gown. I have been writing quite furiously ever since, but am beginning to feel drowsy, so I think I will stop soon. It is past eleven-thirty, and I am looking forward to a peaceful night.

Robert, of course, has already appeared with hot chocolate, which I am still sipping. After that gargantuan meal, I have no appetite for biscuits, but the cocoa is delicious. We did not have much time to talk, because one of the other passengers is feeling somewhat queasy, and Robert was waiting for Dr. O'Loughlin to come up and examine him. However, in the morning, I am sure we can—

A very strange thing just happened. My hand seemed perfectly steady, and yet I spilled part of my hot chocolate. It was as though there was a jolt, and the hot liquid just slopped right over the edge. Perhaps the seas are beginning to get rough?

Oh, I hope not, after such a tranquil time so far.

I am afraid Mrs. Carstairs will be upset when she finds out that I have stained my new nightclothes with chocolate. Maybe I should put them to soak in a washbasin, and change into my old nightdress from St. Abernathy's.

There seems to be some commotion out in the alleyway, so maybe I will go see what happened. Maybe other people noticed the jolting sensation as well?

I have just returned, after shrugging on Father's wool coat as a dressing gown and slipping into my button-boots. People were walking by on their way to the deck to see if perhaps we struck another ship. Others feel that we may have grazed an iceberg, as the weather is so cold tonight. I knocked on Mrs. Carstairs's door, but she told me she was trying to sleep, and I should do the same, as any sensible person would at this hour. I am, however, inclined to get dressed, and go up to the deck to examine the situation for myself. I know he is busy, but I am even tempted to go find Robert, and ask him if — wait, something is different. I am not sure what, but everything seems different.

There has been a change in the atmosphere that I cannot quite distinguish. My ears feel a little hollow, and — *that* is the difference. I can no longer hear the soothing, constant vibration of the engines. Over the past few days, that has become a comforting background noise — and now, just like that, it is gone. I wonder why.

Voices out in the hall keep saying the word "iceberg," but no one seems upset. Maybe this sort of event is routine in ocean travel. It seems odd that the engines would stop, so I hope they are not damaged in any way. Maybe they are just running more slowly, which is why I can no longer hear them.

I think I will go out and find Robert now, since I know that he will relieve my curiosity.

This must be routine. What *else* could it be?

Monday, 15 April 1912

My hands are shaking, I feel hot tears struggling against my eyes, and I have no idea where to begin. I feel a driving need to tell everything *properly*, exactly as it happened, but my mind is cluttered with confusion, and exhaustion, and despair. And *grief*; I am overcome by grief.

The Boat Deck. I will go back to the Boat Deck, and follow the evening through from there. Or — no, the story begins earlier, so that is where I will start.

It was after midnight, and I could still hear people moving about in the passageway. Before I had time to go out and join them, there was a sharp knock on my door. I opened it to see Robert. He was smiling, but his eyes looked urgent.

"Good evening, Miss Brady," he said. "You need to put on something warm, and report to the Boat Deck with your life belt."

Miss Brady? When I heard that, I felt alarmed for the first time, but I was also startled. Had I done something to offend him? That would be terrible. I must have looked upset, because he reached out to pat my arm.

"A routine drill," he said. "No need to fret."

I knew he needed to get on with his duties, so I found a smile for him and nodded. If he said it was routine, it must be routine. Robert started for the next stateroom, but then stopped.

"You'll not want to take your time, Margaret," he said in a very quiet voice.

It did not seem possible — but maybe this was *not* a drill.

"Robert," I started.

"Please," he said. "There's no time to waste."

He looked so worried that I did not want to trouble him with any questions, so I just nodded.

"I have already woken Mrs. Carstairs, but you will want to urge her along," he said.

I nodded again, and he patted my arm once more before moving on to the next stateroom.

My hands trembled as I swiftly pulled on my warmest clothes. My button-boots, the thickest petticoat, the grey skirt, a white blouse, and my old brown sweater. Over all of this, I wore Father's black wool coat, tucking gloves into one pocket, and this diary into the other. On further reflection, I slipped his copy of *Hamlet* in as well, and checked to make sure Mummy's locket was safely around my neck. Then I pulled my life belt over my head and fastened it securely. The belt was so bulky that it was hard to walk, or even move my arms.

Across the hall, Mrs. Carstairs was vexed at the prospect of going outside.

"Why on earth are you so bundled up?" she asked me. "They are merely taking precautions."

If Robert wanted us to hurry, I trusted that he had a good reason. "I believe you should approach this situation as though it were serious," I said calmly. "We must do as we have been instructed."

"Well, I hope they lock the staterooms," Mrs. Carstairs grumbled. "I have far too many valuables to risk."

We had a short argument when Mrs. Carstairs decided that she did not want to expose Florence to the cold night air, and that she should remain resting safely in the cabin. I would not hear of that, and put Florence into her sweater at once. Mrs. Carstairs found this cheeky; at the moment, I found *her* downright stupid.

Mrs. Carstairs also balked at putting on her life belt, because it seemed too cumbersome. I was losing patience by now, but fortunately Robert came in just then and took over, giving quiet, but firm, instructions.

"Will my valuables be safe?" Mrs. Carstairs asked. "Ought we not go to the Purser?"

He told her not to worry, because he would be certain to secure the cabins, and that she must now go to the Boat Deck without further delay. As we were leaving, I looked at him, still smiling but looking very pale in his white uniform jacket.

"Everything will be fine, Margaret," he said. "The crew is terribly well trained."

Surely that must be so, but why was he avoiding my eyes? "Should we wait for you?" I asked.

He shook his head.

"Then you will join us up there?" I asked.

"Straight away," he said.

Still, I felt hesitant. "Ought I to stay down here and help you? I could—"

He shook his head more firmly, and Mrs. Carstairs sighed.

"All right, come along, Margie," she said. "The sooner we go up, the sooner we can come back down."

Robert was nodding, so I bent to attach

Florence's leash and lead her upstairs.

"Just one more thing," Robert said, and then he reached out and checked to make sure that I had fastened my life belt properly. Then he pointed me in the direction of the Grand Staircase and lifts, and hurried off down the hall as a bell rang in one of the other cabins.

"This is utterly ridiculous," Mrs. Carstairs sniffed, as we started up the Grand Staircase, accompanied by a stream of passengers in various states of dress. "We should never have been roused from our beds like this."

"Has this ever happened to you before?" I asked. "You and Mr. Carstairs have taken so many trips."

"In the middle of the night?" she said. "Certainly not! I find it *outrageous*, frankly."

The steps seemed somehow crooked, and I could not figure out why. Was something on the ship broken? How could any of this *possibly* be routine? My heart began to pound, and I was finding it a little difficult to swallow.

On the whole, the other passengers seemed to think this was either a jolly game, or an irritating inconvenience. There was no running or pushing, or even any raised voices. Mostly, people were just joking or grumbling. I relaxed a little, deciding that there must be no good reason to be afraid.

When we stepped outside, the sudden exposure to the icy air made me suck in a short breath. Then again, how could anyone think that the ship would hold a routine *drill* when it was this cold? Such an event would be sheer madness. There must be something terribly wrong here.

"I wonder how soon they will let us go back downstairs," Mrs. Carstairs groused.

"This is absurd. The White Star Line will certainly be hearing from *me*," someone else was saying behind us.

The ship's officers and seamen were uncovering the lifeboats and hurling the canvases aside. The passengers were standing in small groups, watching with perfunctory interest and chatting among themselves. A number of people had merely tossed coats on over their nightclothes and wore slippers on their feet. Since they all seemed to expect to go back inside momentarily, I assumed that my nerves must only be a result of my inexperience.

But if that was so, why did the deck seem to tilt forward? Surely, it ought not to do that. Then again, the *Titanic* was the finest and safest ship ever built, so there must be a reasonable explanation.

The officers were calling for people to board the lifeboats, but almost no one volunteered. The *Titanic* was so warm and safe, with its bright lights, and the dark ocean looked lonely and dangerous. For the time being, it seemed the better part of wisdom to stay aboard.

I saw Captain Smith pass by, with ship designer Andrews, and they were both so carefully expressionless that once again, I felt a stirring of fear. If there was no problem, they would have been making reassuring remarks, and their faces would lack that tightness. Mrs. Carstairs interpreted their calm manner to suggest that everything was perfectly fine, and most of the people around us agreed with her.

I wished that Robert would come out here soon. It was so dark, and crowded, that I was going to have to keep out a very sharp eye for him. There did not seem to be any cabin stewards out here yet, so they must still have had things to do below decks.

In the meantime, the officers at the lifeboats were trying very hard to convince people to get aboard. A brave few did so, which encouraged others to follow along. But the first boat appeared to be barely half full. I was sure that there were plenty of boats, so this did not concern me. We would all have our chance.

A tremendous amount of steam was bursting noisily out of the funnels above us, and I felt a surge of hope, even though it made my ears hurt. Maybe they were getting ready to start the engines again!

Someone was saying that a great crush of ice had fallen upon the aft decks, and that some of the third-class passengers had come up to play an impromptu game of football with the chunks. A few first-class passengers wandered down in that direction to watch, and maybe collect some ice for themselves.

Mrs. Carstairs, who was among the impractically dressed group, shivered next to me. "I cannot be bothered with this tomfoolery," she said. "I am going inside to get warm."

Faint music was coming from the First-Class Lounge, where the band must have been playing. Tentatively, I started to follow her.

"No, you stay out here, M. J.," she said, "so you can come and report on the progress."

So I stayed outdoors. I was on the port side, and the officers were repeatedly requesting that women and children *only* step forward. The first boat on our side was slowly filling up, and the second was being lowered to the next deck, so it would be easier to board. A group of women and children were ushered downstairs to meet it. No sooner had they gone than they returned, because the Promenade windows had blocked their way. So the boat behind it began to be loaded, instead.

The passengers were still very quiet, waiting cooperatively to be told where to go, and what to do. The only shouts came from the men manning the lifeboats, who yelled things like, "Lower away!" and, "We need an able-bodied seaman over here!" and the ever-present, "Women and children first!"

The forward tilt of the deck was, to my eyes, growing more and more pronounced. I could think of no explanation, unless — but we couldn't actually be *sinking*, could we? Suddenly, there was a blinding white light and a strange whistling sound, followed by the boom of an explosion up in the sky. The noise made everyone duck, and now I saw fear in formerly confident faces. My heart was pounding harder than ever, and my stomach began to ache.

"Distress rockets," someone murmured.

Distress rockets?! Impossible as it seemed, that could only mean one thing.

Immediately, I went inside to tell Mrs. Carstairs, and try to convince her to come back out. I was having little success, but then Mr. Hollings came over and echoed my concerns, and she peevishly returned to the Boat Deck. I took hold of Florence's leash and went after them.

"Is there *really* a problem here?" she asked Mr. Hollings.

He glanced around, and then nodded slowly, as though making sure no one else was listening. "The word came down from Mr. Ismay himself, I heard.

You must find yourself a seat, at once." Ismay was the Managing Director of the White Star Line, who I had been told was traveling on this voyage. He would be one of the people most likely to know the true extent of the damage.

Now Mrs. Carstairs's eyes widened, and she allowed Mr. Hollings to guide her over to Boat 8. The boat was already partially occupied, and women were hesitantly stepping inside. An elderly woman allowed an officer and a strapping sailor to help her aboard with her maid. Then, just as suddenly, she got back out and went to stand next to an elderly gentleman still on the deck, saying something to the effect of, "Where you go, I go." Her husband, and the men nearby, tried to dissuade her, but she could not be convinced to leave him behind. So the men turned their attention to her husband, suggesting that he get in the lifeboat as well. He refused them with quiet good humour, and the next thing I saw was the elderly couple going off to sit down in deck chairs. They were holding hands tightly, and seemed unaware of anything in the world beyond each other.

We were sinking. We were *actually sinking*. My legs felt weak, and I had to swallow hard to keep my expression as calm and brave as everyone else's seemed to be.

The officers were still trying to fill Boat 8, and Mr. Hollings implored Mrs. Carstairs to do as they were advising and climb in.

"I–I don't know," she wavered. "It seems so very dark out there. Perhaps I should—"

Was there really time to squander quibbling right now? After all, the word had come from the Managing Director himself, hadn't it? "Just *get in* the boat, Mrs. Carstairs," I snapped.

She stared at me, looking confused.

"Mrs. Carstairs," I said again, through clenched teeth. "Get in the—"

Before I could finish, she nodded shortly and moved toward the boat with something of an offended flounce.

"Here you go, ma'am," one of the officers kept saying patiently, as he tried to coax people into the lifeboat. "Step aboard, ma'am. Women and children only, sir."

Husbands and teenage sons were escorting their wives and sisters forward, and then calmly promising to join them later on. Some of the women meekly obeyed; others refused to leave at all. I saw a couple of women literally being *dragged* into lifeboats, sobbing, while their husbands stayed behind, smiling wanly.

And yet, there was still no real sense of panic. I could not tell whether this was because so many did not want to believe that there was any genuine danger, or if everyone was just extraordinarily courageous. I, for one, was growing increasingly frightened.

Halfway into the lifeboat, Mrs. Carstairs stopped short.

"Wait! I'll not go another step without her!" she cried out.

Mr. Hollings and the nearest officer looked at me expectantly. Without a word, I held out Florence's leash, and Mrs. Carstairs scooped her up and clutched her against her life belt.

"Wait until the other first-class ladies board, dear," she said to me over her shoulder. "Then come along, and we will meet up later."

I had been on the verge of stepping in after her,

and this caught me off guard. *Should* I let the others go first? Considering my station, maybe it would be better to wait my turn. Maybe it was only right. Besides, I had not seen Robert up here yet. I certainly did not want to leave until I was sure that he was safe, too.

"Come on!" the officer said to me, his temper starting to fray. "There's no time to waste!"

I shook my head and stepped away, doing my best to melt into the crowd. I think Mr. Hollings tried to follow me, but it was easy to elude him with the confusion of people milling about, and the deafening explosions of the distress rockets still being fired into the air.

There were plenty of other boats; I would wait my turn.

Later

Writing about all of this is very difficult. There really are no words to describe what those hours were like. I cannot bear to talk, or eat, or — most of all — *think*. And yet, what can I do *but* think?

At the time, I remember feeling dazed, but also

curiously alert. The boats were being loaded, and what had previously been casual partings, with promises to meet up soon, were now wrenching, tearful farewells. Most of the people on the deck seemed to be first-class passengers, and I wondered where everyone else was. Probably there were more lifeboats back on the poop deck, or some other convenient place. There seemed to be a limited number up here, and so many people still needed to be taken to safety. I knew almost nothing about ship procedures, but was sure that they would have planned for a situation like this as a matter of course.

That *did* make me wonder why it was necessary for women and children to go first. If there was room for everyone, the officers should just load the boats without any form of selection. There must be something going on that we had not yet been told.

A number of passengers and crew members were watching the lights of what seemed to be a nearby steamer. A ship must be coming to rescue us! The distress rockets worked! *That* was why the officers were allowing the lifeboats to be lowered away with empty seats. They knew that we would all soon be saved. But, as the moments passed, the lights did not seem to be moving. If anything, they appeared farther away. Now some people were saying that the lights were only stars, or maybe the northern lights, and that there was no ship out there at all. Because if there *was* a ship nearby, how could it not respond to the distress rockets?

The band had come out onto the deck, and was playing a series of light, spirited tunes. By now I was so afraid that my mind was jumbled, and I could not concentrate enough to listen. The feeling of collective fear on the deck was starting to spread, and I felt as though I had to escape from it. I would go find Robert, and wait with him. I walked slowly toward the aft staircase against the steadily increasing flow of nervously chattering people coming outside.

There were still people mingling in the foyer and other common rooms, but most of the alleyways were deserted. I passed a man wearing what might have been a cook's uniform, and reached out a hand to stop him.

"Do you know where I would find the cabin stewards?" I asked.

He glared at me. "The cabins are *locked*, miss. Go back up to the Boat Deck!" Then, without waiting to see what I was going to do, he continued past me.

I noticed how steep the angle of the floor was, and quickened my pace. The ship was *sinking*, and if I tarried down here much longer, I might well sink right along with it. I would just check our row of staterooms, and then I would head back out. Maybe Robert and the others were on the Promenade, or helping out on the poop deck—if only the ship were not so incredibly *big*; it was impossible to find anyone.

I checked every alleyway I could find on C Deck, but never saw a soul. Was I the last person still below-decks? Would all the lifeboats go without me? Fighting a sudden rush of panic, I was turning to hurry back to the aft staircase when I saw someone in a white uniform jacket just up ahead of me. Robert! He was sitting down on the carpet, his back against the wall, staring bleakly at nothing. A life belt was lying next to him, but he made no move to put it on.

"Thank goodness I found you!" I said. "Where have you been?"

He stared at me, looking shocked. "Margaret, I thought you'd left! What are you doing here?"

"Looking for *you*," I said. "Come quickly, it's not safe to be down here."

He looked at me, and his young, sweet face seemed positively ancient. "Please go back upstairs right away, Margaret. Your place is on the Boat Deck."

My place. My place because I was female, or because I was, by a mere technicality, first class? Or was my place waiting to make sure others boarded before I did? Or, tonight, should "place" have been the most irrelevant thing in the world? Somehow, things I accepted my entire life no longer made any sense to me.

"Robert —" I began.

"Go on with you, now, and don't worry about me," he said, looking straight ahead. "There isn't a moment to lose."

Nothing — not even the great welling fear inside of me — would have allowed me to walk away and leave him there alone. I carefully sat down next to him, my balance unsteady on the sloping floor.

"Where are the other stewards?" I asked tentatively.

He shrugged, staring straight ahead. "Gone, I guess. Maybe having a bit of a nip for courage."

"Gone to the other boats?" I asked.

Now, he looked at me with those ancient eyes. "What other boats?"

"Well, there are not nearly enough for everyone on the Boat Deck," I answered. "So I assumed that—"

"There are no other boats," he said.

I blinked, trying to figure out what that meant. "How can that—there are still so many people aboard. How will they get off safely?" But then I knew the answer before he even said anything: They *would not* get off safely. *I* would probably not get off safely. The enormity of this was hard to take in, and I had to close my eyes.

It was very quiet. Sometimes I could hear running footsteps, or the unexplained creak of metal, but there was no rushing of water. We must still have been a few decks above the worst of it.

Robert let out his breath. "You know, you never told me how old you are, Margaret."

"I will be fourteen in October," I said. Except that now I was unlikely to *see* October.

"For me, it would have been seventeen, in August," Robert said.

Would have been? God help us.

Then Robert held his hand out. "Please allow me to take you back upstairs now."

I let him help me to my feet. "I insist that you put on your life belt, first, sir."

Robert smiled, although his lips were trembling. He fumbled for the life belt, and fastened it around his waist. I reached over to tug on the strap and make sure it was tight enough — which made his smile widen. "Now, come on," he said, "while there's still time."

I knew that it might already be too late, but he was right — we had to try. The staircase was so crooked at this point that we both kept stumbling, but finally we made it up to the deck.

"I'll see you off here," he said. "Are you sure you know where to go?"

I stopped to look at him, stunned. "What do you mean, 'see you off'? You need to come with me!"

Instead of answering he reached into his pocket and handed me a White Star envelope, with an address written clearly across the front. "Could you post this to me mum? In case I don't get a chance?"

I just stared at him in horror.

"*Please* don't argue, Margaret," he said. "Go find a boat, quick as you can. I could never rest, knowing otherwise."

I stood there like a right fool, not sure what to say or do.

"Please, Margaret," he said. "I do not want to be worrying about you."

I remembered another dark night when my brother had said, "*Please*, Margaret," in that same desperate way. "What about you?" I asked, hearing my voice shake.

"I have to go find my mates, so we can all give it a go together," he said. "On a night like this, the crew stays together."

The deck had tilted so badly now that it was hard to keep our balance, and I hung on to his arm.

"Please, Margaret," Robert said again, his eyes

staring intensely into mine. "I do not want to beg you."

Although it sickened me somewhere deep inside, I nodded—and saw his face relax.

"Good," he said. "Now my mind will be easy." He put his hand out and touched my face for a moment. "Would you mind doing me one small favor?"

"Anything," I said quickly, hoping he would ask me to *stay* here with him.

He grinned at me. "I should like to remember I kissed a pretty girl tonight."

I nodded shyly, and he gave me a small peck on the lips. This was all new for me, and I was not sure if I was supposed to respond in kind.

"Have you ever kissed a lad before?" he asked gently.

I shook my head, abashed. "No. I am afraid that was not very satisfactory."

He brushed a small piece of hair away from my face. "So, we'll give it another go, eh?"

This time, our kiss was warm and tender.

Robert hugged me very tightly, and then stepped back, looking pleased. "You're a *natural*, Margaret," he said. "I'd better find my mates now. Promise me you'll go straight to the boats."

I swallowed hard, but nodded.

"So, I have your word," he said.

I nodded, as tears filled my eyes.

"Don't worry, love," he said. "I'll be fine." He touched my cheek one last time, and then was gone before I could stop him.

Wherever he went—wherever he *is*—I wish him Godspeed.

Still later

I was crying, but I returned to the lifeboat area. I had promised, so that was what I did. There were still plenty of passengers around, most of them men, but the boats all seemed to be gone. I swallowed, knowing that I had missed my opportunity and would now have to take my chances along with the people who remained. I should *never* have allowed Robert to leave, as we could have tried to swim to safety together. But—I had promised.

For now, I sank into an empty deck chair to

absorb the inevitability of my fate. The bow seemed to be almost underwater, so it would not be long now. The orchestra was still nobly playing away, and I took great comfort from listening to the music. I thought momentarily of writing in this diary, but instead, I took out *Hamlet* and began to thumb through the pages.

"Margie-Jane!" a deep voice said. "What are you still doing here? I was certain you and Mrs. Carstairs had long since left."

It was Mr. Prescott, who had dined with us, along with his wife, so many times during the voyage. I scarcely knew him, but it was wonderful to see a familiar face.

"She left earlier," I said. "Where is Mrs. Prescott?"

His expression tightened, and I deeply regretted having posed the question at all.

"I sent her on ahead," he answered. "Now, come, quickly, to the Promenade with me. We may just have time."

We hastened down there and I saw a number of women and children climbing across a bridge of deck chairs to get into a lifeboat. There *was* one left. I felt elated — and inconsolably guilty at the thought of getting aboard.

"You and the men —" I started.

Mr. Prescott cut me off. "We have no time for idle chatter, please, just come along." Then he raised his voice. "Let us through, please, gentlemen! I have a young girl here!"

Men moved aside, without the slightest thought for themselves. There are not sufficient words in the English language to honor their valor and gallantry, but I will never forget it — any of it — as long as I may live.

Colonel Astor was there, helping his young wife across the treacherous bridge of chairs. I heard him ask if he could stay with her, due to her condition, but the officer refused him. The Colonel accepted this gracefully, and asked the number of the boat, so he would be able to find her in the morning. Then he moved away, his dog Kitty trailing behind.

A woman was trying to board with her children, but the officers stopped her son and told him to go back and stand with the men. A man who must have been his father protested that the lad was only thirteen. The officer in charge scowled, but let him pass.

Another woman was clutching her young son. Then he was wearing a woman's hat—I am not sure who put it on his head, but it may have been Colonel Astor. After that, she and her children were allowed aboard with no comment from the officers. I wished so very much that Robert would find his way here; at only sixteen, they might relent and let him board as well.

Except that I knew they would not, and *he* would not.

"Quickly now," Mr. Prescott said to me. "We mustn't hold things up."

I did not know what to do, but found myself impulsively hugging him.

"You are a perfect gentleman, sir," I said, "and a credit to us all."

He smiled, and let his hand rest gently on my head for a second. "Come on now, child, it's time. Mind the chairs."

Then, just like that, I was half-climbing, and half-falling, into the lifeboat. I recovered my balance, and made my way to a seat in the bow. As I sat down, the cry to "Lower away!" went up, and my end of the boat dropped toward the water. Next, the bow dropped, and we continued in that erratic fashion.

The last thing I saw was Kitty—noble in her own right—staying close by her master's side.

The *Titanic* was so low in the water that we had a very short trip down. We made balky progress, and one of the two sailors aboard reached for a knife to cut us free. But then we hit the water, and were able to cast off. The portholes were still brightly lit, but I could see water rising unchecked through C Deck and making its inexorable way upward.

"My God," a woman near me whispered. "She really is going down."

All around us, heavy objects were crashing into the ocean. At first, I feared that the remaining passengers on the ship had gone mad, but then I understood that the deck chairs and other wooden articles could be used for flotation devices.

We had only two men aboard, so another sailor came sliding down the davit ropes to join us. Several more followed in his wake, landing heavily in the boat. A number of women were knocked down and badly bruised as a result.

Anyone who was near an oar grabbed hold and started rowing. I was too far forward to be of any help, and besides, I was unable to take my eyes off that beautiful stricken ship in what appeared to be her death throes.

"Row with all your might!" a man was yelling. "Before we get sucked under!"

First they rowed one way, and then we reversed direction. I had no sense that anyone was in charge. Two men who had taken a chance and jumped off the ship now swam towards us, their arms flailing wildly. They were hauled aboard, shivering from just that brief period in the freezing water.

Even then, to my amazement, I could hear the brave sound of violins being played aboard the ship. As the bow began to disappear completely, there was an enormous din of shattering glass and crashing metal from inside the ship. People were leaping into the water from all directions, while others scrambled toward the stern in a frantic, hopeless attempt to save themselves.

No one in our boat spoke, or perhaps even *breathed*. The horror of these last moments was too awful to watch, but it was impossible to look away. Several women gasped as the *Titanic*'s front funnel suddenly ripped free and smashed violently into the water, and then her stern rose higher in the air.

I am not sure if the engine rooms had exploded, or if the ship broke in half—but amidst all of the crashing noises, the bow had gone under, and, slowly, the stern was lifted straight up into the sky. I could hear distant screams as people were thrown off, or else struggled to hang on. The ship's lights were abruptly extinguished, and then came back on for one final second before we were all plunged into utter darkness.

The clamor of smashing, crashing, tearing metal seemed endless. The stern stayed straight up in the air like that, a stark shadow against the stars, for what seemed like an hour, but may only have been a minute. Then, with an almost stately grace, it gradually slipped beneath the surface of the ocean.

The *Titanic* was gone.

Tuesday, 16 April 1912

Carpathia

I had to stop and return to my diary in the harsh light of day because the next part is the worst of all. After the *Titanic* sank, the unspeakable shrieking of hundreds of people dying filled the night. Frenzied, terrified screams. Since we were still very close to where the ship had sunk, I could distinguish individual voices begging for help, calling out for people they loved, and praying for salvation.

"We must go back," one of the women in my boat said, her voice shaking. "We must help them."

"We can't!" another woman shouted, nearly hysterical. "They'll kill us all! No one can help them anymore — we have to save ourselves!"

Everyone chimed in with their own opinions — I was very much in favor of returning — and a near-mutiny ensued. Finally, a ship's quartermaster named Perkis made the decision that we were so close we had to try. He said that he was in charge, and we would follow his bidding. So our boat began to row back, and we were able to pull five or six half-frozen men out of the water. Each time, I prayed that one of them would be Robert, and each time, my prayers were not answered. One of the men was clutching a bottle of brandy, and Quartermaster Perkis tossed it overboard, since the man was obviously *already* intoxicated and might become unruly.

The rescued men were drenched, and a goodly amount of water had spilled into the boat as we struggled to haul them in. It was deep enough to cover my boots completely. Most of the men were in a very bad way, and I offered the one closest to me my coat. He was too cold to respond, so I just took it off and covered him as well as I could.

The screams of the dying seemed to last forever. It was a horrifying, unearthly sound that would have sickened the very Devil himself. I am not sure which was worse: the screams themselves, or the way they gradually faded away. I think we had enough room in our boat to try to rescue a few more — but now, we were rowing in a different direction, and the quartermaster could not be persuaded otherwise. The rescued men's teeth were chattering, and some of them were out of their heads from the cold.

Other than trying to help them get warm, no one knew what else to do.

It was pitch-black, except for the stars, and even Quartermaster Perkis did not seem sure about which way we should go. As far as I know, we were just rowing around in circles. After a while, we heard a whistle blowing, and rowed towards it. A boat commanded by an Officer Lowe wanted as many lifeboats as possible to tie up together for safety. I think there were three other boats who responded to his call, and Officer Lowe transferred all of his passengers into our boats. He was planning to return to the site where we had last seen the *Titanic*, and try to rescue some more people.

While we waited for him to return, our boats drifted aimlessly. There were a number of children, as well as a few babies, on our lifeboat, and some of them cried on and off. Obviously, there was no milk to give them to soothe their distress. I tried to help one woman by rocking her baby for a while, but had no more success calming him than anyone else had. Between the crying babies, a few seasick women, and the ravings of the frozen men — one of whom was also very drunk—ours was not a quiet boat.

On the whole, I do not remember any conversations. There may have been some, but I just cannot remember. I think I just sat there in utter despair. Two of the women near me were weeping, but most had been silenced by a combination of grief, shock—and the terrible cold. Anyone who was not fortunate enough to be rowing, which served as an excellent distraction, just hunched down and tried to stay warm. At some point, two of the men we had pulled aboard succumbed to their ordeal, and died. After that, the silence aboard our boat was impenetrable.

Officer Lowe returned with only four more survivors—all of them strangers—and then directed us to begin rowing again. A sailor caught sight of another boat with figures standing up on it. He said that it was one of the collapsible emergency boats, and she looked to be in grave danger of capsizing. With Officer Lowe's encouragement, we rowed over there with one other lifeboat—Boat 12, I think. Between us, we were able to take on all eighteen or twenty men. Again, Robert was not among them. Maybe he was on another lifeboat, or was clinging safely to some wreckage, or — I could not face the other possibility.

By now, our boats were very crowded and the water inside reached to my knees. Had the sea not been so calm, we would surely have been swamped.

When a passenger first shouted that she saw a ship, none of us believed her. The men told her that it was probably only a shooting star, or maybe dawn beginning to break. But as the lights loomed closer, we realized that it *was* a steamer, and she was heading our way!

For the first time, we all had a feeling of hope. The sky was getting brighter, and the steamer was still coming towards us. As a new morning dawned, the sky pink and light blue, I was stunned to see that we were surrounded by a veritable mountain range of icebergs. In the dark, they had been completely invisible, but now they were everywhere. For objects so lethal, they were also majestic, and almost beautiful in a horrid way.

Someone in our boat checked her watch, and announced that it was going on to five in the morning. I felt as though our time in the boat had lasted for months, so I was surprised only a few hours had passed.

The rescue steamer proceeded cautiously through the ice field. Every so often it would stop to take aboard the occupants of a lifeboat. Our boat rowed doggedly in their direction, but we did not get to her side until almost eight o'clock. Up close, I could see that our saviour was called the *Carpathia*.

There were ladders, and cloth slings, hanging over the side to help us aboard. Many of the people in our boat were too weak to climb, but I chose a ladder. As I reached the deck, a uniformed man helped me aboard. As he asked me my name and wrote it down, a woman pressed a mug of hot liquid into my hands and wrapped a blanket around my shoulders. I lurched off to the side, out of the way, so that others could also come aboard.

A great many survivors were waiting by the railing, searching for loved ones and friends. We were one of the last boats to be picked up, so I knew that their hopes were growing faint. My legs were shaking, so I sat down on the deck, and sipped the hot liquid. The taste was unexpected, but I recognized the smell as coffee. There may have been some brandy in there as well.

A kind-faced woman knelt next to me and offered to show me to the saloon, so I could get warm. Once in there, someone else handed me a sandwich, and my mug was refilled. By and by, a doctor stopped to examine me, and pronounced me perfectly fit, and extremely lucky. I was none too sure of the former, but utterly certain of the latter.

I must say that the commander of the *Carpathia*, Captain Rostron, was terribly heroic. Having seen those treacherous ice fields, I have no idea how he made his way to us without his own ship crashing. Once all of the lifeboats had been emptied, he steered his ship over to the area where the *Titanic* had gone down, in search of more survivors. Alas, there were none to be found, and there was not even much debris to be seen.

Another ship, the *Californian*, arrived around then, and they were to continue the search while we headed for New York.

Before we steamed away, Captain Rostron gathered all of us together for a brief service. He and a reverend gave thanksgiving for the approximately seven hundred of us who had been saved, and then led us in prayer in memory of the more than fifteen hundred people who had been lost.

Fifteen hundred.

As soon as I felt stronger, I began to look around to see if anyone I knew had survived. There were *so few* men, and I never found Robert. Or Mr. Prescott, or Mr. Hollings, or Ralph Kittery, or so many others. Colonel Astor had not survived, and neither had Mr. Andrews or Captain Smith or Dr. O'Loughlin or — my mind just could not accept the enormity of the loss of all those fine people.

Especially, of course, Robert. I *should never* have left him alone like that, no matter how hard he begged. Surely, if he was brave enough to accept his fate, I should have been as well.

I think the *Titanic*'s crew may have suffered the most devastating percentage of deaths. Stewards, cooks, engineers, postal workers — even the entire band perished. How admirable they were! How admirable *all* of them were!

Steerage passengers also fared far worse than

the rest of us, although those in the second class had a great many die, also. I am sure there were countless stories of heroism among their ranks, which will never be told, as so few eyewitnesses are alive to tell them.

This afternoon, I was sitting out on the deck half asleep, when I heard a familiar bark. I opened my eyes to see Florence tugging at her leash, and trying to pull Mrs. Carstairs in my direction. Mrs. Carstairs saw me, and looked very pleased.

"What an agreeable surprise!" she said. "I was so very concerned. Now that I have found you, you must come and join me for the rest of the voyage."

I shook my head, too exhausted and sad to face that notion. "Thank you, but I would rather be alone just now."

She stared at me, dumbfounded. "But —"

"Robert died," I said, and came very close to bursting into tears.

She nodded, her expression more serious than I had ever seen it. "I'm sorry, child. I know how fond you were of him."

I nodded, and rubbed my hand across my

eyes, trying very hard not to cry. To my surprise, Mrs. Carstairs dragged over a deck chair — by herself! — and sat next to me.

"My Frederick would have died, too," she said. "With Thomas Prescott, and all of the others. And *I* would have been on that lifeboat, thinking that he would be perfectly fine."

We were now safely on a ship, surrounded by widows; she was, indeed, lucky Mr. Carstairs had not made the voyage. We sat in silence, for there seemed to be little to say.

Then I let out my breath. "Thank you," I said. "For *I* should have been in steerage." And therefore, almost certainly would have also died in those icy waters.

Mrs. Carstairs nodded, set Florence on my lap, and we sat there together without speaking for the rest of the afternoon.

Wednesday, 17 April 1912
Carpathia

We are supposed to arrive in New York tomorrow night. During the last couple of days, I have done little more than write and think, and think some more. I am not hungry; for the most part, I have not slept.

The *Carpathia*'s passengers have been uniformly sensitive and benevolent. They have donated clothes to those who have none, along with toothbrushes and other necessities. Some of them have even given up their beds! I decided that I would be more comfortable bunking on the floor of the saloon, or outside on the deck. For those of us in that position, the ship provided steamer rugs and blankets to try to make us comfortable.

When my parents died in such quick succession, I thought my whole world had come to an end. I could not understand why they had died, or how life could be so cruel. And now, I do not understand why *I* survived, when so many others did not.

And why did not every single lifeboat return to help our fellow human beings? Had we not already been so close, I do not think *our* boat would have gone back, either. People were too frightened, too confused, too self-protective, to remember others. But, *we had room*. All of the lifeboats did.

Fear seems a paltry excuse. We were *all* afraid that night. I know I did not want to die, but neither did I want to doom others to their helpless, frozen fate.

Although I suppose that is exactly what I did by virtue of taking my seat on Boat 4 in the first place. I doomed Robert; I doomed complete strangers. I hope that I can figure out some way to understand all of this. Why it happened, what could have prevented it, how to keep anything like this from ever taking place again.

Most of all, I hope I can learn how to forgive myself for still being alive, when so many others are not.

Thursday, 18 April 1912

Carpathia

We steamed into New York Harbor at eight-thirty P.M., in the midst of a fierce thunderstorm. Somehow, given the circumstances, that seemed only fitting. Smaller boats surrounded us, and many of the bright flashes we saw came from cameras, not lightning. Then, when we finally berthed, I could see a tremendous crowd waiting for us on the pier.

Before we disembarked, I saw Mrs. Carstairs making her way towards me. Awkwardly, she tried to hand me one of her typical wads of folded bills.

"Here," she said. "I thought you might need this."

I shook my head. "No, thank you. You have already done more than I deserve."

"Take it, it's a pittance," she said, sounding impatient. "My address is there, too, if you need anything."

I hesitated, but then slowly nodded and tucked the bills into my pocket. I was about to land in a foreign country, with no idea of what was going to happen, or where I was going to go — and the few pounds I had had were now at the bottom of the ocean.

"Will your brother be here to meet you?" she asked.

Would he? "Yes," I said, uncertainly. "Everything has been arranged." Of course this was not true, but what did it matter?

She nodded, and then we looked at each other.

"It is not for us to know why we survived," she said. "Try to remember that, Margaret."

I hoped, very much, that that was true.

The gangways had been laid out now, and the first group of numb, tired passengers began to get off. When it came to be my turn, I followed those who had gone ahead, looking neither right nor left. It was a chaotic scene, as people searched for loved ones, and reporters rushed around with notepads, trying to get stories. I ignored all of this, only wanting to get off the pier and find a quiet place to sit down. Mrs. Carstairs had located her son-in-law, and she offered to drive me to the train station or a hotel, but I assured her that I was fine. I thanked her one last time, she shook my hand, and then I bent to give Florence a light kiss on top of the head.

That was the last time I saw them.

Once they had left, I stood alone in the frantic crowd, trying not to panic. Where *was* I going to go? I was in the middle of a strange city, with nothing more than the clothes on my back, and a few dollars. It was upsetting to have so many people swarming around me, and it took me quite some time to make it to a quiet street corner across the way. I wanted to sob loudly, but was afraid of drawing attention to myself.

Gradually, the crowds began to thin out. Every so often, someone would stop and ask me, eagerly, if I had been on the *Titanic*, and I would just shake my head. It was easier that way.

I had so hoped that William would be here, but I did not know where to start looking. For all I knew, he thought I had perished at sea. Maybe he had never even gotten the letter I sent from St. Abernathy's! I did not want to leave, in case he *was* here, but maybe I should go try to find a room for the night. Then tomorrow, I would have to figure out some way to get to Boston.

Slowly, I got up and began to walk around some more. I was still surrounded by strangers, and the whole scene was overwhelming. If I could just sleep for a while, maybe I would feel better, and could think more clearly.

After all, this would not be the *first* time I had slept on the streets.

A woman standing by two tall bundles of apparently donated clothing asked me if I needed help, but I just shook my head. I have accepted far too much charity in my life, and no longer want to do so.

Ever.

I finally found a deserted bench, near the shipping office. At first, I just sat down, but when no one seemed to notice me, I stretched out and closed my eyes.

Maybe when — if? — the sun came up, I would know what to do.

I was sound asleep when I suddenly felt someone sit down next to me, and a hand touched my shoulder. I opened my eyes, terrified — and then recognized my brother.

"There you are," William said, his eyes filling with tears. "I was worried sick."

I began crying, too, and hugged him with what little strength I had left. William hugged back and I rested my head against his shoulder, not even noticing the pouring rain.

I was finally safe.

Friday, 19 April 1912

Somewhere between Boston and New York

After a joyful reunion, William brought me to the small hotel where he had been staying for the last two days, hoping and praying that I would arrive soon. The White Star Line had insisted that I was on the survivor list, but he knew he would not believe it until he actually *saw* me.

He tucked me into bed, and brought me a ham sandwich and a cup of tea. I fell asleep before I could finish either, and did not wake up until almost noon. Once William was sure I was strong enough to travel, we went up to the railroad station to get a train to Boston.

First, though, we posted Robert's letter. I could only hope that it would give his mother some small comfort.

When our train was announced, William helped me board and put his coat over me as a blanket. I had yet to stop shaking since the lifeboat, although I am not sure it had anything to do with cold temperatures.

"It's a miracle that you got here, Margaret," he

said. "Everything will be okay now. I am going to rent us a bigger flat, and with my salary, you can start school soon. I don't want you to have to worry ever again."

I just nodded, and leaned against him, too tired to respond.

Now we are riding along, and I do not even have enough energy to look out the window. I am so very tired and sad. I do not even feel like writing now—and may never again.

Saturday, 20 April 1912
Charlestown, Massachusetts

I think this will be my last entry. Frankly, I am not sure there is anything left to say. The flat is very nice, and we can divide it with a curtain for the time being, so we each have our own room. William looks just wonderful—taller than ever, and full of confidence. I can tell that he is very happy here, and hope that one day, I will be also be happy again.

This morning, after breakfast, William sat back and looked at me for a few minutes.

"Are you ready to talk about it?" he asked.

I shook my head.

"Okay," he said, and cut me another slice of bread.

We spent the rest of the morning sitting quietly and sipping tea. There was no need for conversation; simply being together again was more than enough.

"William?" I asked finally.

He looked up from across the table.

"Would you mind terribly if we got a cat?" I asked.

He studied me for a moment, and then grinned at me. "We can get two," he said.

Tomorrow, we plan to do just that.

It may be a trifling step forward, but it is a step regardless. Part of me would like to stay with my grief forever, but that would not do justice to the sacrifices that have been made on my behalf. As long as I live, I will never forget the great courage shown by Robert and so many others. I only hope that I can live up to their fine example.

I pray they are all at peace.

Epilogue

Margaret Ann Brady never once discussed her voyage on the *Titanic* in public — and also rarely mentioned the disaster in private. Throughout her life, she felt that the memories of those tragically lost were best served by a respectful silence. She also never completely forgave herself for surviving the tragedy.

She *did* permit William to read her diary, and then sent it on to Sister Catherine, who later returned it for safekeeping. Margaret completed her high school education in Boston, and then accepted a scholarship to Wellesley College.

Margaret and Sister Catherine never lost touch, and on two occasions, Sister Catherine was actually persuaded to come visit Margaret in the States. The only time Margaret ever returned to England was for her beloved mentor's funeral in 1962.

Margaret also kept up a regular correspondence with Nora, who later emigrated to the United States with her new husband when she was nineteen. They had a joyous reunion, and Nora ended up settling in nearby Pawtucket, Rhode Island.

After their parting in New York, Margaret and Mrs. Carstairs exchanged letters a couple of times, but never saw each other again.

When the First World War broke out in 1914, William immediately volunteered to fight for his new country. He served valiantly until he was seriously wounded during a trench battle.

Margaret dropped out of college in order to devote her time to nursing him back to health and working to support them. Although William ultimately recovered and got a job with the Boston Police Department, Margaret never returned to college. She did, however, continue reading voraciously.

In 1923 Margaret met a young history teacher named Stanley Ryan at a bookstore in Cambridge. They were married the following June, and spent the next forty-four years laughing and arguing together. They had three children: Dorothy, Harriet, and . . . Robert. Margaret devoted many long hours to volunteer work, helping disadvantaged youngsters in the Boston area, and she later ended up heading a halfway house for unwed mothers until her retirement in 1965.

During her life, Margaret occasionally boarded planes, and regularly took trains — but she refused to set foot on another boat ever again. Despite her many decades in America, she never lost her British accent, but to her surprise, she became extremely fond of coffee.

She died peacefully in her sleep in 1994, at the age of ninety-five.

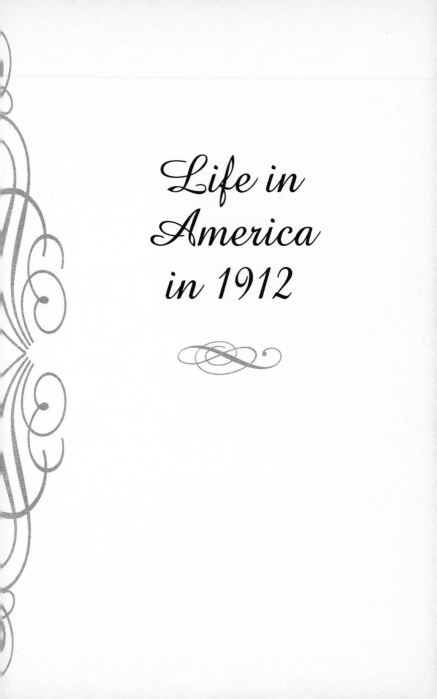

Life in
America
in 1912

Historical Note

Over the years, the tragedy of the *Titanic* has been a source of endless fascination and speculation for people all over the world. The *Titanic* was the largest ship that had ever been built, and such a technological marvel that even a conservative shipbuilder's magazine raved that she was "practically unsinkable."

In the years before the First World War, public confidence in England and America was at an all-time high. King Edward VII held the British throne during this period, and the era was dubbed the Edwardian Age. A general air of complacent confidence prevailed. The *Titanic*, with her glittering passenger list, seemed like the ultimate example of human achievement in this optimistic time.

In 1912, the rich and famous were famous primarily *because* they were rich. Society events were reported in great detail in newspapers and magazines. Ordinary citizens enjoyed living vicariously through these reports.

There was also a very strong class system in effect. Upper-, middle-, and lower-class people rarely came into contact with one another, and would never have interacted socially. Lower- (or working-) class people "knew their place," and thought nothing of being ignored by those they considered to be their "betters." By that same token, members of the upper class looked down upon anyone who was not at their level financially and socially. The upper class was also expected to "set a good example" for others, and this concept of "noblesse oblige" was generally accepted by everyone. Actually, the vast majority of people probably existed somewhere in the middle, but the two extremes got the most attention. These rigid notions of class were much stronger in England than they were in America, but they still existed here.

Throughout the early 1900s, technology and industry were booming. The international shipping business was a particularly competitive field. Speed and comfort were the two most important concerns for any passenger liner. Voyages that had once taken months could now, because of powerful steam engines, be completed in less than a week. As a result, a number of companies were vying to dominate the business. The two best known were the Cunard Line and the White Star Line, which was run by International Mercantile Marine (IMM).

In 1907, Cunard was probably the most successful, with their impressive new ships, the *Lusitania* and the *Mauretania*. J. Bruce Ismay and William James Pirrie, two top IMM executives, decided to meet that challenge by building the three biggest ships in the entire world. They would be called the *Olympic*, the *Titanic*, and the *Gigantic*. The Harland and Wolff shipyard in Belfast, Ireland, was commissioned to do the job. The *Olympic* was launched, to great fanfare, in 1911, and the *Titanic* was to sail on her maiden voyage a year later.

The plan was for the new White Star ships to offer weekly passages from Southampton, England, to New York City. They would be fast, they would be dependable, and they would offer remarkably pleasant sailing experiences.

The *Titanic* was just over 882 feet long and 92.5 feet wide. This length translates to $\frac{1}{6}$ of a mile! She stood well over 100 feet tall, which is the equivalent of 11 stories in a building. She had 9 decks, 3 propellers, and weighed more than 45,000 tons. The decks ranged from the Boat Deck all the way down to the boiler rooms in the bowels of the ship. She was equipped with a total of 20 lifeboats, which exceeded the admittedly minimal standards of the day. Most impressively, the ship had been designed to have 16 watertight compartments in its hull, all of which could be closed individually with the mere flip of a switch. This made the ship unusually safe.

She had a number of features never before seen on an ocean liner, including a swimming pool, Turkish baths, a squash court, a gymnasium, and several restaurants. The ship even had elevators! Second-class accommodations were equivalent to first class on other ships, and the conditions in third class (also known as steerage) were unusually pleasant.

As a Royal Mail Steamer (RMS), the *Titanic* obviously carried countless sacks of letters and postcards. Some of her other cargo and provisions included 40 tons of potatoes, 75,000 pounds of fresh meat, 600 gallons of condensed milk, 15,000 bottles of beer, 5 grand pianos, a marmalade machine, and 12 cases of ostrich feathers.

The *Titanic* also had a crew of approximately 900 (though many of these numbers have never been accurately established). The crew was broken down into 3 categories: the Deck Crew, the Engineering Crew, and the Victualling Crew. These various workers included the Purser, the Marconi wireless radio operators, the saloon and bedroom stewards, postal clerks, cooks, bakers, firemen, engineers, stewardesses, and, of course, the 8 members of the band.

The passenger list included many famous celebrities, including one of the richest men in the world, John Jacob Astor, and his second wife. Other well-known passengers were J. Bruce Ismay, the Managing Director of the White Star Line; Thomas Andrews of Harland and Wolff, who had designed the ship; Mrs. J. J. Brown, known as "the Unsinkable Molly Brown"; Isidor Straus, who had founded the famous Macy's department store in New York, and his wife; and Major Archibald Butt, who was President Taft's top military aide.

Of the estimated 1,320 passengers, many, of course, were not famous at all. While the first class was heavily comprised of socialites, along with their maids and valets, the second- and third-class passengers were more conventional. Second-class passengers were predominantly successful professionals, including teachers, middle-class families, and businessmen. The third-class passengers tended to be immigrants on their way to America to make new lives for themselves. Many of them were Irish or Italian, but other nationalities were represented, too.

At noon on April 10, 1912, the *Titanic* prepared to cast off under the command of Captain Edward J. Smith. Captain Smith was the most popular of all White Star Line officers, and was commonly known as "E. J." After completing the maiden voyage of the *Titanic*, Captain Smith was planning to retire.

A near accident marred the beginning of the *Titanic*'s journey. While being towed away from her Southampton berth by tugboats, the *Titanic* nearly collided with a smaller ship, the *New York*. A quick turn by Captain Smith, along with some swift interference by the tugboat *Vulcan*, prevented a dangerous crash.

Despite this mishap, it was a happy leave-taking, and thousands of people had gathered on the quay to see the ship off. That evening, the ship arrived in Cherbourg, France, to pick up more passengers. Then the *Titanic* steamed toward Queenstown, Ireland, scheduled as its final stop before going to New York City. There were now an estimated 2,200 passengers and crew members aboard.

On Thursday, April 11, the *Titanic* finally headed out to the open sea. The weather was beautiful, if cold, and the early days of the voyage were uneventful. The atmosphere aboard the ship was cheerful and at ease. Passengers spent most of their time eating fantastic meals, relaxing, and exploring the ship.

Then disaster struck on the night of April 14, 1912. The seas were remarkably calm, but before retiring for the night, Captain Smith instructed First Officer Murdoch to watch out for ice and "alert him" right away if anything happened.

At 11:40 P.M., Lookout Frederick Fleet saw a huge iceberg loom up out of nowhere. He instantly alerted the officers in the bridge. With barely thirty seconds to make a decision, Officer Murdoch ordered "hard a-starboard!" and tried to steer out of the way, but the starboard side of the *Titanic* scraped violently against the iceberg. Metal tore, rivets popped, and water began rushing through the hull of the ship. It had been a glancing, but ultimately fatal, blow.

Captain Smith instantly came to the bridge and summoned ship designer Thomas Andrews to go below and inspect the damage with him. Andrews came to the quick — and tragic — realization that the *Titanic* would sink within the next hour or two.

In the meantime, most of the passengers and crew were unaware of the seriousness of the situation. Many passengers noticed a slight "bump" or "jarring" or "scraping," and some were even awakened from a sound sleep. But since they assumed the *Titanic* was unsinkable, almost no one was terribly concerned.

Around midnight, Captain Smith gave orders to uncover the lifeboats and load the women and children first. There were over 2,200 people aboard, and at full occupancy the lifeboats could carry only

1,178. Captain Smith and his fellow crew members tried very hard to keep this information from the passengers, to prevent panic. In order to keep up morale, the band, led by Wallace Hartley, began to play. With total disregard for their own safety, they continued to play on the Boat Deck until the very end.

Wireless operators Phillips and Bride were busy sending out "CQD" and "SOS" distress signals. Many ships responded, although most of them were too far away to be able to help. The *Carpathia*, about 58 miles away, immediately began rushing to the rescue, but it would take her several hours to arrive. Perhaps the most controversial aspect of the disaster concerns a nearby ship, the *Californian*. She may have been as close as 4 or 5 miles away, although this exact distance has never been established. Her radio operator had gone to bed, so she never got the distress calls — nor did she respond to the distress rockets the *Titanic* began shooting into the sky.

Throughout the night, the *Titanic*'s passengers and crew members were — with very few exceptions — remarkably brave in the face of danger. Men routinely stepped back and gave up their lives in order to save women and children. In some cases, wives stayed behind with their husbands in a courageous example of the "till death do us part" marriage promise. There are many wild legends of officers firing guns to keep frantic passengers at bay, and men dressing as women in order to sneak onto boats — but there is really no way of knowing exactly what occurred. White Star Managing Director Bruce Ismay took a place in one of the last available boats, and was condemned as a coward for the rest of his life.

Once the last lifeboats were gone, there were still about 1,500 people aboard the *Titanic* — almost all of whom were now doomed. The bow was completely underwater, and the ship was sinking rapidly. Captain Smith told his crew that they had performed nobly, and that it was "every man for himself." He was never seen again. During all of this, the band kept playing. Their selfless devotion to duty is one of the most inspiring stories to come out of the tragedy.

At about 2:15 A.M., the ship snapped in two and the bow slipped under water. Slowly, the stern of the ship began to rise up into the air. The front funnel broke off and slammed into the water, crushing a number of people who were trying to swim away. The stern stood up in the air until it was almost exactly perpendicular, and then it, too, disappeared beneath the water's surface.

It was 2:20 A.M. and the *Titanic* was gone forever.

Even though many of the lifeboats had room for more people, *only one* made a point of going back to pick up survivors. That boat found only four people left alive, one of whom died later.

At about 4:30 A.M., the *Carpathia* steamed up, after a risky journey through dangerous fields of ice. Her commander, Captain Rostron, demonstrated astonishing seamanship and grace under pressure. The survivors were brought on board, and the *Carpathia* set sail for New York City. Just over 700 people survived, while more than 1,500 perished.

The night the *Titanic* sank was one of darkness and courage, nobility and despair. For the most part, the very best of humanity was on display—with the very worst of results. It is a night that will never be forgotten.

The Titanic's planned voyage included a return trip from New York on April 20, 1912, as indicated in this advertisement by the White Star Line, the shipping company that owned the Titanic.

Southampton, England, the port of origin for the Titanic, *was a working-class town much like London's East End. The children seen here may have worked in the shipyards or on the ships, or had parents who did so. Though much has been said of the* Titanic's *wealthy passengers, many working-class families from England, Ireland, and other European countries also boarded the* Titanic *in hopes of finding a better life in America.*

The Titanic *was unveiled at Southampton port. At 882.5 feet from bow to stern and decorated with the finest furnishings of the period, she was the largest and grandest ship of her day. Even in a city where people were accustomed to seeing large ships, the* Titanic's *maiden voyage was an exciting event, and families lined the dock to see her set sail.*

One of the early indicators that this would be an ill-fated voyage was the Titanic's *near collision with another ship, the* New York, *just moments after leaving the dock at Southampton. The tug boat is leading the* New York *out of the* Titanic's *path.*

Captain Edward John Smith was the commander of the Titanic. This was supposed to be his final voyage before he retired from a 38-year career as a ship's captain with a perfect sailing record. Ironically, it was his final voyage, because the captain went down with his ship.

Second-class passengers take a stroll on the promenade deck. The first-class promenade was a separate area behind these passengers, more toward the Titanic's bow. The third-class promenade was at the stern. Passengers in each class were kept separated, as was customary at the time.

The Grand Staircase, graced by a glass dome overhead, marked the entrance to the first-class passenger areas.

Meals at sea were an event, and in first class, passengers had several dining options—from a casual café that younger passengers enjoyed to this more formal dining room.

A typical luncheon menu included several courses. This was the last luncheon served in first class before disaster struck.

A first-class bedroom typically included a bed, sofa, wardrobe, vanity, and washbasin, though some first-class passengers did share a washroom. There were also staterooms, which included a separate sitting area. Few children traveled in first class, but those who did shared suites with their parents. In third-class bedrooms, children slept in bunk beds.

The first-class reading and writing room on A Deck offered passengers a place to read, play cards, or write letters. Children met their friends here or played games outside on the deck.

One of the most famous areas of the ship was the gymnasium, which was complete with one of the first stationary bicycles. Another favorite spot was the Titanic's swimming pool, where, for 25 cents, passengers could purchase a ticket to swim.

The Titanic's mail room workers (pictured here) and other crew members had the least luxurious quarters. Theirs were located on the lowest decks, which partially accounts for the high death rate among the crew.

Telegrams were sent from and received by the Titanic's *wireless room (shown here). Ships' wireless rooms are often called Marconi rooms, named for Guglielmo Marconi, the man who manufactured telegraph equipment.*

POSTAL TELEGRAPH — COMMERCIAL CABLES

TELEGRAM 79

```
280  Wy.Rn.  22

S S Amerika via S S Titanic and Cape Race N.C. April,14,1912

Hydrographic Office,Washington DC

Amerika  passed two  large icebergs in 41 27 N 50 8 W on the 14th

of April

                    Knutp,10;51p         62496   HYDRO OFFIC
                                         filed with  Rec'd APR 15  1912
                                         2-995              Enclosure.
```

At 1:45 P.M. on April 14, 1912, a German ship, the Amerika, *sent a telegram to the* Titanic *warning of ice in its path. Many other ships sent ice warnings, too. Because ice was common in the area, the warnings were not considered serious.*

This dramatic painting shows lifeboats being lowered into the water. Unfortunately, many passengers were not aware of the grave danger, so several lifeboats were only half-full.

When they reached the site of the Titanic's accident, passengers on other ships in the area took photographs of the iceberg they thought caused the disaster. A smear of red paint runs along the base of this iceberg, leading observers to believe that it had been struck recently.

There are no photographs of the Titanic as it sank. Many artists have rendered paintings based on eyewitness testimony.

One of the Titanic's *four collapsible lifeboats was photographed by a passenger on the* Carpathia, *the first ship to arrive at the scene.*

Still dressed in their formal evening clothes, rescued Titanic *passengers recover on the* Carpathia's *deck.*

This is one of the few photographs taken of surviving third-class passengers.

Early reports indicated that the Titanic *had been damaged but would arrive in New York as planned. This newspaper headline reveals the devastating truth.*

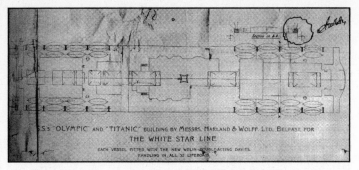

This diagram shows the original plan to include 32 lifeboats on the Titanic. However, according to British Board of Trade regulations in 1911, only 16 lifeboats were necessary. The shipping company voluntarily added 4 more collapsible boats, bringing the total to 20. Inquiries into the accident later revealed that it would have taken 63 lifeboats to save all of the Titanic's passengers.

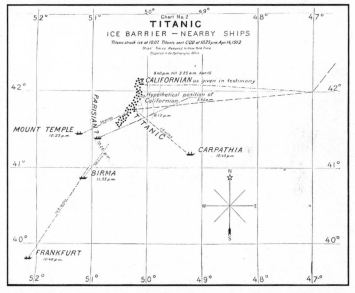

Both American and British authorities conducted investigations of the Titanic disaster. Key issues were the number of lifeboats, the reliability of the telegraph equipment, and the location of other ships that were sailing nearby, as shown on this map. In the end, it was determined that no one person or thing was to blame; rather, it was a series of unfortunate occurrences that led to the most well-known maritime tragedy of all time.

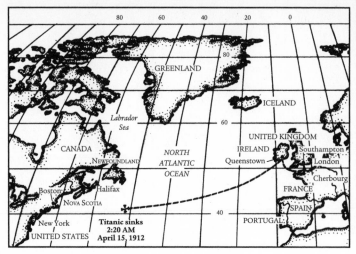

This map charts the Titanic's *ill-fated course.*

Timeline

1898: A writer named Morgan Robertson publishes a story called *Futility*. It is a prophetic tale about a ship, named the *Titan*, that hits an iceberg and sinks on its very first voyage. The ship does not have enough lifeboats, and many of its passengers die.

1907: The International Mercantile Marine Company, known as IMM, is being run by J. Bruce Ismay, who controls the White Star Line of ships. He and William J. Pirrie, head of a construction company called Harland and Wolff, decide to build two new ships, the *Titanic* and the *Olympic*.

1909: Construction begins on the *Titanic* at a Harland and Wolff site located in Belfast, Ireland.

May 31, 1911: The *Titanic* is launched for the first time.

January 1912: Sixteen lifeboats are installed on the *Titanic*. She has the capacity to handle many more, but the law in Britain does not require them. The *Titanic* is also provided with four collapsible lifeboats.

March 31, 1912: The *Titanic* is fully outfitted and ready to commence her maiden voyage as the largest and most luxurious ship ever built.

April 2, 1912: Tests (known as sea trials) are conducted on the *Titanic*. They are completed in about half a day. That evening, the ship departs for Southampton, England.

April 3, 1912: Cargo and supplies are loaded onto the ship in Southampton, and the first crew members are hired.

April 6, 1912: The rest of the crew is hired, many of them local residents of Southampton.

April 10, 1912:

> **7:30 AM**: Captain Edward J. Smith, who will command the ship, boards the *Titanic*.
>
> **8:00 AM**: Two lifeboats are tested in a short drill.
>
> **9:30 – 11:00 AM**: Second- and third-class (also known as steerage) passengers begin to board the ship.
>
> **11:30 AM**: Boarding begins for first-class passengers.
>
> **Noon**: The *Titanic* sets out on its maiden voyage, but is delayed by a near collision with a much smaller ship, the *New York*.
>
> **6:30 PM**: The *Titanic* arrives at her first stop, Cherbourg, France, and almost 300 more passengers are ferried to the ship. She is an hour late.
>
> **8:10 PM**: The *Titanic* heads for its next stop — Queenstown, Ireland.

April 11, 1912: The *Titanic* has traveled 386 uneventful miles in near-perfect weather.

April 13, 1912: The superb weather continues, and the *Titanic* completes another 519 miles.

> **10:30 PM**: Another ship, the *Rappahannock*, sends a warning of severe ice.

April 14, 1912:

9:00 AM: An ice warning is received from the *Caronia*.

11:40 AM: Another ice warning comes from the *Noordam*.

1:42 PM: Yet another ice warning is sent by the *Baltic*.

1:45 PM: Still another ice warning arrives, from the *Amerika*.

7:30 PM: Three iceberg warnings are sent by the *Californian*.

9:20 PM: Captain Smith goes to bed, ordering Second Officer Lightoller to wake him if there are any problems.

9:40 PM: Another ice warning comes in, this time from the *Mesaba*.

10:00 PM: First Officer William Murdoch relieves Lightoller on the bridge.

10:55 PM: The *Californian*, only a few miles away, tries to send another ice warning, but the overworked *Titanic* telegraph operator tells them to "Shut up!"

11:30 PM: The telegraph operator on the *Californian* signs off for the night.

11:40 PM: *Titanic* lookouts Fleet and Lee spot a large iceberg in the calm ocean and call down to the bridge. Officer Moody tells them, "Thank you." Officer Murdoch, who is currently in charge, is unable to steer out of the way, and the starboard side of the ship is torn open in the resulting crash.

11:50 PM: The first five compartments of the ship are filling with water, as is Boiler Room 6. (A stubborn coal fire that raged in the Boiler Room may have weakened its strength.)

April 15, 1912:

Midnight: Captain Smith and Thomas Andrews, the builder of the ship, go on a quick tour to inspect the damage. Andrews estimates that the *Titanic* will sink within two hours. Captain Smith has distress calls sent to nearby ships with the message that the *Titanic* is going down and is in desperate need of help. Responses begin to come in from everyone except the nearby *Californian*. Initially, Operators Phillips and Bride use the traditional "CQD" signal. Later, they switch to the new "SOS."

12:05 AM: Captain Smith orders that the lifeboats be readied and that all passengers put on their life belts. If fully loaded, the lifeboats can carry only 1178 people. There are approximately 2200 people on board the *Titanic*.

12:15 AM: The *Titanic*'s band begins to play "lively" music to help prevent a panic.

12:25 AM: The lifeboats begin to be loaded with women and children.

12:45 AM: The first lifeboat — Lifeboat 7 — is lowered away, holding only 28 passengers. It has room for 65. Simultaneously, the first distress rocket is fired, as the *Titanic*'s officers try to get the attention of a ship (thought to be the *Californian*) that they can see in the distance.

12:55 AM: Lifeboat 7 leaves, with Lifeboat 5 soon to follow. The boats are still not fully loaded.

1:00 AM: Lifeboat 3 leaves.

1:10 AM: Lifeboat 1 leaves. It has only twelve passengers aboard. It can hold forty.

1:15 AM: The *Titanic* is visibly sinking.

1:20 AM: Lifeboat 9 leaves, more fully loaded than any boat so far, but still not filled to capacity.

1:25 AM: Lifeboat 12 leaves.

1:30 AM: Lifeboat 14 leaves.

1:35 AM: Lifeboat 13 leaves.

1:40 AM: Collapsible Boat C leaves, with J. Bruce Ismay boarding at the last minute. He is later heavily criticized for this.

1:45 AM: The *Titanic* sends out its final message to the *Carpathia*. Lifeboat 2 leaves.

1:55 AM: Lifeboat 4 leaves.

2:05 AM: Almost all of the lifeboats have gone. Collapsible Boat D is being loaded with women and children.

2:17 AM: Captain Smith releases the crew from their duties and tells them to try to save themselves, since nothing more can be done. Collapsibles A and B are washed overboard by the rushing water. Later on, survivors will cling to them.

2:20 AM: The *Titanic* sinks. Approximately 1500 people — passengers and crew — die in the disaster.

3:30 AM: Lifeboats spot rockets being fired by the *Carpathia*, which is speeding to the rescue.

4:10 AM: The *Carpathia* picks up passengers from the first lifeboat it encounters, Lifeboat 2.

8:30 AM: After several hours of rescue work, the final lifeboat, Lifeboat 12, is picked up. At the same time — hours too late to help — the *Californian* appears.

8:50 AM: The *Carpathia* sets out for New York City with an estimated 705 survivors aboard.

April 18, 1912: The *Carpathia* arrives in New York.

April 19 – April 25, 1912: Under the committee leadership of Senator William Smith, the United States Senate conducts hearings to investigate the sinking.

May 2 – July 3, 1912: A similar inquiry, run by British authorities, takes place in England, attempting without much success to assess blame for the disaster.

April 1913: The International Ice Patrol is formed in the hopes of preventing another tragedy like the *Titanic*. It is administered by the United States Coast Guard.

November 1955: *A Night to Remember*, by Walter Lord, is published. More than fifty years later, it is still considered the best book ever written about the *Titanic*.

September 1, 1985: American scientist Dr. Robert Ballard and his crew, along with French scientist Jean-Louis Michel, discover the wreck, lying more than two miles below the ocean's surface.

July 1986: Dr. Ballard explores the wreck and takes underwater photographs of it. Out of respect, he makes no attempt to retrieve anything, and hopes that no other expedition ever does so.

There have been a number of dives since Dr. Ballard's discovery. Crews have recovered everything from dishes to clothing to furniture.

About the Author

In the course of her research, Ellen Emerson White found many accounts of the *Titanic*'s voyage from the first- and third-class points of view. Because the classes never mingled, she thought it would be interesting to explore the privileged experience of the wealthy through the eyes of a working-class girl who, by a stroke of luck, finds herself traveling in first class.

Ms. White has written several critically acclaimed novels for young adults, among them *The President's Daughter*, *Life Without Friends*, and *Long Live the Queen*, which was named an ALA Best Book for Young Adults. For Scholastic Press she has written *The Road Home*, also an ALA Best Book for Young Adults. She lives in New York.

Acknowledgments

Grateful acknowledgment is made for permission to use the following:

Cover portrait by Tim O'Brien.

Cover background: *Titanic*. © Popperfoto/Getty Images.

Page 185: White Star Line advertisement, Hulton Archive/Getty Images.

Page 186 (top): Northam Street Scene, Southampton, England, Southampton Maritime Museum.

Page 186 (center): Titanic at Southampton, Mariners' Museum, Newport News, Virginia.

Page 186 (bottom): Near miss with the *New York*, Mariners' Museum, Newport News, Virginia.

Page 187: Captain Edward J. Smith, Popperfoto/Getty Images.

Page 188 (top): Passengers strolling on deck, Cork Examiner, Ireland.

Page 188 (bottom): The Grand Staircase, Mariners' Museum, Newport News, Virginia.

Page 189 (top): First-class dining room, Mariners' Museum, Newport News, Virginia.

Page 189 (bottom): Luncheon menu, Southampton Maritime Museum.

Page 190 (top): First-class bedroom, Mariners' Museum, Newport News, Virginia.

Page 190 (bottom): First-class reading and writing room, Mariners' Museum, Newport News, Virginia.

Page 191 (top): Gymnasium photo, *L'Illustration*, from *Titanic: Triumph and Tragedy* © 1994 by John P. Eaton and Charles A. Haas, published by W.W. Norton, Inc. Reprinted by permission of the authors.

Page 191 (bottom): Mail room workers, from *Titanic: Triumph and Tragedy* © 1994 by John P. Eaton and Charles A. Haas, published by W.W. Norton, Inc. Reprinted by permission of the authors.

Page 192 (top): Wireless room, Express Newspapers, Photo by Father Browne/Universal Images Group/Getty Images.

Page 192 (bottom): Telegram from the *Amerika*, National Archives, Washington, D.C.

Page 193: Lifeboat painting, Hulton Archive/Getty Images.

Page 194 (top): Iceberg, Mariners' Museum, Newport News, Virginia.

Page 194 (bottom): *Titanic* sinking, © Ullstein-Willy Stoewer/The Image Works.

Page 195 (top): Survivors in lifeboat, Mariners' Museum, Newport News, Virginia.

Page 195 (bottom): Survivors on board the *Carpathia*, North Wind Picture Archives, Alfred, Maine.

Page 196 (top): Third-class passenger survivors, *New York Evening Journal*, from *Titanic: Triumph and Tragedy* © 1994 by John P. Eaton and Charles A. Haas, published by W.W. Norton, Inc. Reprinted by permission of the authors.

Page 196 (bottom): Newspaper boy, Topical Press Agency/Getty Images.

Page 197 (top): Lifeboat diagram, National Archives, Washington, D.C.

Page 197 (bottom): Diagram of nearby ships, National Archives, Washington, D.C.

Page 198 (top): Map of voyage by Heather Saunders.